"There's only one reason a woman wants a fake boyfriend..."

"To make her friends jealous." Colton waited a half second, his eyes glued to Ashley's. When she didn't move, didn't shove, didn't object in any way, he lowered his mouth to hers and kissed her.

This was not the kiss she'd expected.

This was slow. Leisurely. Like he enjoyed getting to know her mouth. Like he wanted to explore her lips, the inside and outside of them. Not to mention deep inside her mouth. His big hand cupped the back of her head and he tilted her—gently—one way and then the other, as he slanted his mouth over hers. When he finally pulled away, she was left, lips parted, panting.

"That ought to do it."

She blinked once, twice, three times before coming back to herself, suddenly cluing in to the fact that the whistles and catcalls were because of the show they'd put on.

Oh, shit.

What had she done?

Dear Reader,

Have you ever done something completely out of character? Acted (or reacted) spontaneously in a moment of passion, fear, joy or anger? What was the repercussion of that act? Did it turn out okay? Did you regret it? Did it take you down a path you never thought you'd ever take?

Personally, I've never done anything out of character...

Yeah, right! Of course I have. Everyone has. For example, there was this scuba instructor I met while vacationing in the Philippines... What should have been a simple holiday fling turned into me moving to Berlin with him on a whim... Ahem. Crazy, right?

Did it work out in the end? No. Do I regret it? Nope. Not one bit, because while we weren't a forever match, I learned so much about myself through that relationship.

In *Wild Seduction*, Ashley Ozark does something in the spur of the moment, too, something wild and crazy, something completely out of character. Does she regret it? You bet. At least at first because *accidentally* making out with the least likely man possible and pretending he's her boyfriend challenges everything she believes about herself, her hometown and the type of man she wants as a lover. Does her impulsive act turn out okay? Well, you're just going to have to read to find out!

On that note, I hope you enjoy *Wild Seduction* and fall in love with Colton Cross as much as Ashley does—even if she doesn't want to. I love to hear from readers, and I would love to hear some of your stories. Just drop me a line to say hi at dairestdenis@dairestdenis.com.

Happy reading!

Daire St. Denis

Daire St. Denis

Wild Seduction

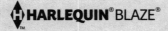

HARLEQUIN® BLAZE®

Recycling programs
for this product may
not exist in your area.

ISBN-13: 978-0-373-79963-3

Wild Seduction

Copyright © 2017 by Dara Lee Snow

www.Harlequin.com

Printed in U.S.A.

New York Times and *USA TODAY* bestselling author **Daire St. Denis** is an adventure seeker, an ancient history addict, a seasonal hermit and a wine lover. She calls the Canadian Rockies home and has the best job ever: writing smoking-hot contemporary romance where the pages are steeped in sensuality and there's always a dash of the unexpected. Find out more about Daire and subscribe to her newsletter at dairestdenis.com.

Books by Daire St. Denis

Harlequin Blaze

Sweet Seduction
Big Sky Seduction
A Christmas Seduction

To get the inside scoop on Harlequin Blaze and its talented writers, visit Facebook.com/BlazeAuthors.

All backlist available in ebook format.

Visit the Author Profile page at Harlequin.com for more titles.

EVERYTHING LOOKED BETTER behind the lens of a camera. Ashley Ozark focused on a group at the end of the bar, and the shutter of her Canon EOS 5D Mark III made a delightful swish as she captured a head thrown back in laughter, a sardonic look from a friend, another face shadowed by a cowboy hat and a fourth wiping his brow. She smiled, happy with the result of the image, a conversation between friends and rivals, so intimate she almost felt like she'd overheard it.

She knew those men, rodeo boys, probably egging each other on, making bets, relieving tension before the county fair and rodeo this weekend.

A sharp-nailed, *rat-a-tat-tat*, on the top of her head made her lower the camera.

"Ouch."

Her older sister, Beth, stood to her side. "You're supposed to be helping bartend tonight. Not spending the entire time behind that camera."

"I've been hired to take pictures by the County Fair Committee. I'm just doing my job here."

"Yes, and you've also been hired to tend bar tonight." She indicated the long line of patrons waiting to be served. "By our father, I might add, who is also on the Fair Committee."

"Okay, okay." Ashley sighed, tucking the camera away

into its bag and storing it under the counter. "I got some great candids in here."

"I'm sure you did." Beth tossed an apron at her head, but Ash caught it before it hit her face. "Now put that on and get to work."

"Tyrant," she muttered.

"You got that right."

"Bully."

"Exactly. Now get to work before I kick your ass."

"Like you could."

With a grin, Ashley tied the apron around her waist and lifted her chin at the next person in line, indicating she was ready to take their order. While she helped out at the bar on the odd occasion because the Prospector Saloon in the Gold Dust Hotel was owned by her family, it really wasn't her scene. She preferred her quiet job at the flower shop, Heart's Bouquet, down the street. However, during the county fair it was a given—all hands on deck. That meant all five of the Ozark girls were required to help: she and Beth behind the bar, Brandi on the floor and the twins, Zoe and Chloe, in the kitchen. This year it was even more imperative because it was Half Moon High's Centennial celebration, so they expected more out-of-towners than normal. Based on the crowd tonight, it was an accurate assumption.

Ashley was happy to help. It meant extra dough, both working at the saloon and taking pictures, and every penny she made was going toward her Get-the-hell-out-of-Half-Moon Fund. So she plastered on a smile and kept the cold ones coming. Already the bar was standing room only, even though the festivities didn't officially start until tomorrow. The din from people talking and laughing was so loud, it drowned out the sound of the band. That was until her sister Brandi got up on stage between songs and grabbed the mic.

"Good evening, ladies and gentlemen," she bellowed and yet still managed to sound sultry in a way that only Brandi could with her practiced, husky voice.

People stopped talking and heads turned—or at least, every *male* head turned, like a flock of sheep.

Baaaaa.

"For those who are visiting, welcome back to Half Moon Creek. We're so pleased you were able to come to the rodeo and fair this year and to celebrate Half Moon High's Centennial Celebration. We'll be kicking everything off Friday morning—Oh, my God! That's tomorrow, already—with a parade followed by the rodeo and opening of the fair grounds. Don't forget to pick up tickets for Saturday's big formal banquet. Tickets are still available at the front desk and…"

"Sweetheart?" came a voice from her left. "A little help here. I've been waiting for fifteen minutes and…"

Ashley spun toward the deep voice. She turned up the volume on her smile when she saw who it was. Colton Cross. Figured. The cocky, bull-riding cowboy was exactly the kind of person who would think it was okay—no, not okay—he probably figured she'd be *flattered* by him calling her sweetheart.

"Well now, *honey baby*. What can I get for my *sugar pie*?"

"What?" Colton mouthed the words *sugar pie* with a look of confusion on his unfortunately handsome features.

"Oh. I'm sorry, *sweetie*, aren't we on a 'terms of endearment' basis?"

"Umm…" Colton's brows drew together so close they formed one line across his forehead. "Ahh…whatever you say, darlin'. Can I get two pints of Beaverhead draft and an order of nachos—"

"You did not," Ashley said, leaning across the bar. This

was exactly why she couldn't wait to leave Half Moon. Macho rodeo jerks like Colton Cross.

"I did not, what?" He asked slowly.

She rolled her eyes. "Call me *darlin'*—"

Oomph.

Beth elbowed Ashley out of the way.

"Hey, Colt," Ashley's oldest sister said with a genuine smile, while inconspicuously giving Ashley a side kick to the butt. "Don't mind my sister. She's weird."

"*She's* your sister?" Colton said, looking back and forth between Beth and Ashley and then glancing over his shoulder at Brandi who was still on stage talking animatedly about some of the highlights of the weekend.

"There are two more of us hiding out around here, somewhere." Beth gave a vague wave toward the kitchen. "Five Ozark girls in total."

"Wow. I did not know you two were sisters." He glanced at Ashley again, who was openly scowling at him because, seriously, the fact that Colton Cross had *no* idea who she was only confirmed her opinion of him: self-centered, chauvinistic, thickheaded…oh, she could go on. Egomaniac, cocky, disgustingly good-looking…

"Didn't you two go to grade school together before you moved?" Beth asked.

"Yep." Ashley said the word, short and clipped, giving him the coldest look she could muster. By the way he tilted his head to one side and then the other as he gave her a quick once over, she knew he had no recollection of her. Zip. No memory of Valentine's Day in fifth grade when she'd gone and made him a special Valentine and he'd repaid her by spitting in her hair later that day in the playground. Didn't matter that her family had known his family for years or that ever since he'd returned to Half Moon a few months ago to help his brother out at his guest ranch, he'd been the talk of the town. Well, the talk of the female population, anyway.

"Oh yeah," Colton said slowly, covering up the fact he couldn't place her. "Nice to see you again... *Bren-da*, right?"

Nice try, hotshot. "It's Ashley."

"Right. Now I remember."

As if.

She poured the beer and slid the frosty glasses across the bar. "Tab?"

"Yes, please. Oh, and about those nachos...?"

She nodded and, without another word to him, rang in the order and then began serving the next customer in line.

"Try to be a little nicer," Beth whispered in her ear.

"I am nice," Ash said through clenched teeth.

"No, you're ornery."

"So?"

"So, the nicer you are, the more tips you make." Her sister eyed her apparel and sighed. "It doesn't hurt to flirt a little either, which would help because that outfit isn't doing a thing for you."

"Thanks. I appreciate the vote of confidence," she muttered beneath her breath.

Once Beth turned her attention to the next customer, Ashley glanced down at her well-worn jeans and T-shirt with the slogan Well Behaved Women Seldom Make History. It was one of her favorites. Plus, it could be interpreted as flirty, couldn't it?

"Boo!"

It took Ashley a few seconds to recognize the woman who had jumped into her line of sight. Not because she didn't know her—she had been Ashley's best friend for her entire high school life—only because she hadn't seen her in five years, and Jasmine Sweet was the *last* person Ash expected to see tonight.

"Jazzy?"

Her friend waved her arms in the air. "In the flesh!" She squealed, hopped up onto the bar—which was a maneuver that did not jibe with the designer clothes she was wearing—slid across to the other side, hopped down and enveloped Ash in a bear hug, making Ash's eyes water from the combination of the fierceness of the embrace and the floral perfume that floated around Jasmine like the sweet scent of honeysuckle on a summer's eve. Or...like a cloud of gnats before a rainstorm.

Ashley patted Jasmine's back until the woman finally let up, stepping back and smiling down at her, which was odd because she and Jasmine had always been the same height.

Short. Or, *fun-sized*, as Jasmine called the two of them.

"Look at you! You haven't changed a bit," Jasmine gushed.

Ashley was going to say, "Neither have you." But it would have been a lie. Jasmine had changed since she'd managed to escape Half Moon a week after graduation. She'd always been beautiful, but now she looked *different*. She was sophisticated, with her expert makeup and hair pulled back in a chic ponytail. Ash realized the height difference was due to a pair of red, high-heeled shoes that perfectly matched Jasmine's designer handbag. Her clothes were clearly expensive—tailored black capris and a sheer sleeveless top in white that accented her dark skin tone—simple and elegant while still being sexy.

She was the same old Jasmine, only improved—vastly—with age.

"You look amazing," Ash said, wiping her suddenly sweaty palms on the front of her old jeans. "What are you doing back here?"

"What do you mean?" Jasmine's dark eyes glowed with excitement as she glanced happily around the bar. "I'm here for the same reason everyone else is. To see old friends and to celebrate the centennial, Half Moon style!" Her laugh was infectious, as always.

"Wow." That's all Ash could come up with, still in a state of disbelief by Jasmine's unexpected arrival.

"How long has it been?" Jazz asked before holding up a hand to stop Ash from answering. "No, wait, don't tell me, it'll only make me feel like a terrible friend." She leaned close in order to whisper in her ear, "We have so much catching up to do."

"Yeah," Ashley murmured, smoothing her own haphazard ponytail, awkwardly.

"But first—" Jasmine took in the lineup of patrons waiting to be served "—you look like you could use a little help behind the bar."

"Oh, no," Ash protested, assessing Jasmine's outfit and deeming it too put-together to be worn by a bartender in a busy saloon where it would undoubtedly get messed up. "Really, you don't need to do that."

"Did someone just offer assistance?" Beth sidled over, grinning broadly as she inserted herself between Ash and her friend.

"Beth!" Jazz squealed and gave Beth a hug.

"Was Ash surprised?" Beth asked.

Ashley blinked at her sister. She knew Jazz was coming and didn't tell her?

Beth read her thoughts—as only Beth could—and said, "Jazz called to say she wanted to surprise you." She winked. "By the expression on your face, I'd say Jazz got you pretty good."

"She sure did. Wow." Ash cringed internally. Really? Was that all she could come up with? Wow?

Slinging her arm over Jasmine's shoulder, Beth said, "And you are even more gorgeous than ever. Seriously, Jasmine, what's your secret?"

"No secret. Chicago agrees with me, I guess." Waving

her hand at the crowded bar, she asked, "Please, tell me I can help back here."

"Of course you can."

The next half hour was a blur of pouring drinks and taking orders and trying to keep all the bar tabs straight, but with Jasmine's help, things went more smoothly and the tip jar was soon filled to overflowing. It didn't hurt that Jasmine knew pretty much everyone and chatted them up in typical *Jazzy* fashion, as if she truly cared about each and every one of them.

Through it all, Ashley only spilled two drinks, one on herself and one on Jasmine.

"Oh, my God," Ash cried, trying in vain to wipe the beer off Jasmine's blouse. "I'm so sorry. This is probably really expensive."

Jasmine only laughed as she took the cloth from Ash and blotted the stain in an equally ineffective manner, probably because the cloth was covered in beer, too. "It's no big deal. Hazards of the job, right?"

That's when Ashley noticed Jasmine's hand. Or rather, the big, fat diamond ring adorning the ring finger of Jasmine's left hand. Ash grabbed her hand to take a closer look. "You're engaged?" She rubbed the stone. It was huge, something a celebrity might wear.

"I am." Jasmine beamed. "His name's Parker, and we've been living in sin for two years, so we figured it's time."

"Wow."

C'mon, Ash. Plenty of words in the English language.

She cleared her throat. "Where'd you meet?"

"Chicago. At this party. It was really posh and I totally felt out of place." She leaned close to Ash and whispered, "He said I was the most exotic woman he'd ever met." She giggled. "Me. Little old Jasmine Sweet from Half Moon Creek, exotic? Can you believe it?"

This time Ashley managed to contain the *wow* that sat

tingling on the tip of her tongue. "He's obviously got good taste."

Jasmine squeezed Ashley's fingers. "I was going to call to tell you, then I thought, why not come and tell you in person instead?" She opened her mouth in a silent, happy scream, and a second later, Ashley found herself crushed once more in Jasmine's arms, the wet patch on Jasmine's blouse soaking into the only dry patch on her T-shirt.

"I'm happy for you," Ashley said. "Really happy."

"You want to see a picture?"

"Of course."

Jasmine fished her phone out of her pocket and flipped through the photo app. "Oh, here's a good one."

Holy shit. Parker wasn't just good-looking, he was… perfect. Perfect blond hair. Perfect clothes that were trendy and fit him…perfectly. Straight white teeth showing up in his perfect smile.

"He's very…handsome." Ash handed the phone back to her friend, who stuck it in her pocket again. "You must be very happy."

"I am." Clapping her hands with glee, Jasmine gushed, "But do you know what would make me happier?"

Ash slowly shook her head. Was it possible for someone to be happier than Jasmine currently was? Was it even fair?

"If *you* help me plan it." She shivered. "Oh, it'll be like old times. Say yes."

"Of course." Ash pulled her lips back in what she hoped resembled a smile of sorts.

They went back to serving drinks, and, if at all possible, Jasmine served with even more vigor than before. In fact, her energy was in direct proportion to Ashley's sudden lack of enthusiasm, to the point where Beth asked her what her problem was.

"No problem," Ash snapped.

With arms crossed over her chest, she studied her. Narrowing her gaze, she glanced at Jasmine, then back at her. "Take a break."

"No—"

Her sister took hold of her by the shoulders. "Your shirt is a mess." She touched her hair. "This is a mess." Using her chin she indicated the back of the saloon. "I've got a makeup kit and a stack of extra shirts in the office. Go get yourself sorted."

"Fine."

Ash slipped down the bar toward the door to the kitchen. Her skin felt tight, every inch of her sensitive to the sogginess of her shirt, the tickle of errant wisps of hair against her face, the cinch of her belt.

What was wrong with her?

Jasmine's laugh chased her all the way into the kitchen, nipping at her heels and making her flinch with the cheery sound of it. She paused just inside the kitchen, leaning against the wall. The last time she'd felt this way was the day before Jasmine had up and left Half Moon Creek.

Memories flooded her. The first week as a freshman, when Jasmine's family had moved to town and Jazzy had decided they should be best friends because they were in three out of four classes together. They'd become inseparable after that, hanging out after school, and on weekends. All the important firsts were shared: first time skinny-dipping at the quarry, first time trying cigarettes—Jasmine's idea. First time texting boys—ones Jasmine liked. First dates—Jasmine's. First kisses—also Jasmine's...

Four long years of Ashley living in Jasmine's shadow.

Now, after just an hour, she was right back in it. Only now the shadow was bigger than ever, and Ash wondered if she'd ever see the light of day again.

"What are you doing?" Zoe, the shiest of her shy twin sisters, said. "You look sick."

"I'm fine." Ash gave herself a mental shake and went

on into the office in the back to freshen up. Beth's makeup bag sat open on the desk, and she had a stack of identical black tank tops with the pub's logo on the back sitting on the corner. After stripping off her sticky shirt, she pulled one on.

She checked herself out in the mirror. God, how could Beth wear these all the time? Yes, they were made of that stretchy spandex cotton blend, but Beth had at least two cup sizes on Ash, and the tank top was tight on Ashley. However, right now, tight was better than beer-sodden, so, after unsuccessfully stretching the material—it was like elastic, snapping right back into place—Ashley loosened her hair and ran a brush through it before refastening her ponytail. There was no way she could pull off the sleek, sophisticated look that Jazz had, but at least it was neat. *Neater.*

Never one to wear much makeup, she pored through all the junk in Beth's bag before finding a lip gloss that didn't look too bright and some blush.

There.

She blinked at herself in the mirror.

Marginally better.

"Oh, my God. That's a *thousand* times better," her sister said when Ashley reemerged a minute later.

"Look at you!" Jasmine cried. "God, you are *so* cute." She shook her head in wonder. "I tell you, you are *exactly* the same." She indicated the bar with a sweep of her hand. "Just like this place. I love it."

Something deep in the pit of Ashley's stomach let out a low, menacing growl.

"It's like time stands still here."

Errrrr...

"It's so comforting." Jasmine closed her eyes and smiled. "You have no idea."

The growly thing in her tummy reached up and snagged the inside of her throat, making it difficult to swallow.

"So, tell me, cutie-pie." Because she was wearing high heels, Jasmine had to stoop a little in order to lean Ash's way. "Anyone snatched you up yet?"

The hot, beasty thing inside of her had tentacles, one of which was snaking up her spinal cord and others that slithered into her extremities. Whatever it was, it was intent on possessing her, and the growl in her tummy slipped right out of her throat.

"What did you say?" Jasmine asked with a wrinkle of her nose.

Ash licked her lips, about to embark on a diatribe, about what? She had no idea. "Yeah, I've got a boyfriend."

"You do?"

"Sure."

Someone cleared his throat.

"Hey, honey, about those nachos…?"

Ashley spun. Colton Cross stood there, adjusting his cowboy hat so it tilted back on his thick head. Perfect. "Nachos?"

"Yeah." He squinted.

"You want nachos, *baby*?" She beckoned him closer. "C'mere."

A puzzled expression settled over his features as he leaned across the bar. When Ash fisted her hand in the front of his shirt and tugged, his expression went from puzzled to wide-eyed surprise.

"Look, I'm sorry if I offended—" he began.

She didn't let him finish. For whatever-God-forsaken-reason, Ashley leaned across the bar and planted a juicy one, square on Colton Cross's lips, sucking his apology right out of his mouth before he had a chance to finish.

"What the—"

Her mouth still close to his, she whispered, "Pretend to be my boyfriend, just for tonight, and your nachos and beer tab are on the house."

2

WHAT THE FUCK had just happened? The snippy girl from behind the bar kissed him. Like, full-on, openmouthed kissed him.

"Pretend to be my boyfriend, just for tonight, and your nachos and beer tab are on the house."

"Is this a—" Colton intended to say, "joke," but the girl locked her lips on him once more, shutting him up.

So, Colton decided to roll with it. Why the hell not? Seemed like a decent deal to him, free beer and nachos for a little bit of spit swapping? He pulled away. "As much as I want?"

"As much as you want, what?" she whispered, her face flushed, like she was angry.

Weird chick.

"Beer. Nachos." He wet his lips and was about to say "kisses," because—damn—the girl might be a harpy but she wasn't half-bad in the kissing department.

"Yeah, yeah, whatever." She blinked hard. "No, wait." It was like she was doing a calculus problem in her head, her eyes rolled up and to the side, and her ruby lips moved silently, like she was figuring something out. "Well, within reason. Like you better be legal to drive home to the Silver Tree Ranch afterwards."

"How'd you know where I live?"

"God!" She huffed out a breath and rolled her eyes

again. Whatever he'd done to piss her off was clearly still irritating her, despite her lusty lip on lip action.

"Is this him?"

A dark-haired beauty leaned on the bar, a hand outstretched. "I'm Jasmine. Ashley and I go way back."

Ashley. Right. Good thing the friend mentioned her name, because he'd forgotten it and almost called her Brenda again. He shook the woman's hand. "Colton."

Ashley gave him a fierce look, trying to convey...something. Who the hell knew what this woman wanted? She turned to her friend and said, "Colt and I had a bit of a fight earlier, so..." She shrugged. Like that summed up their whole relationship. Which, as far as he was concerned, it did.

"She was snippy," he offered, helpfully.

She glowered. "You were an ass."

Rubbing his jaw, he said, "Can't say I recall that part."

"We might break up." Her face was red. Not a sweet blushing red, but a fiery red, complete with nostrils flared and steam spewing out of the ears. Angry-bull red.

He chucked her beneath the chin. "She's so funny. It's why I love her."

Her eyes went saucer-sized.

Damn. Too far?

"I mean, I don't *love* her, love her."

Yes. There was the steam pouring out of her orifices again. This was fun.

He flashed a well-meaning Cross family smile at Ashley's friend, who watched their interaction with a little pucker between her brows. Leaning toward her, he said, "I love making her *mad*, is what I mean. She's feisty when she's mad. And when she's feisty...?" He whistled high, then low, hoping the friend would catch his meaning. Shit, this was the easiest free grub ever. "So, babe," he said to Ashley, "about those nachos. I'm thinking a double order for me and the boys at the end of the bar. Sound like a plan?"

"Sure."

"I'm also thinking a couple more makeup kisses are in order, too."

Kaboom.

She was like a cartoon character, blowing her top.

Hands up in mock self-defense, he said, "I'll collect later." He grinned and then wove his way back down to the end of the bar, looking forward to telling the boys how he'd finagled free food for the lot of them.

"Huh," Jasmine said, a wrinkle between her brows as she watched Colton walk away.

Ash rubbed the spot between her own brows in response because she could feel way more than a wrinkle there. A chasm.

Jesus, Mary and Joseph. What the hell had she done?

"Well," Jazzy's frown slipped away to make room for a huge smile. "He is one hot tamale." She leaned close and whispered, "How's the sex?"

Ash choked on her spit. Her sister, very helpful sister that she was, smacked her hard between the shoulder blades. A couple good hard whacks. Then, when Ash finished choking, she leaned down and hissed in her ear, "I told you to *flirt*, not *make out* with the customers."

Ash gave Beth a meaningful look. At least her sister got her looks. Unlike the dolt she'd chosen to be her pretend boyfriend.

Coughing once more, Ashley said to Jasmine, "Sex is super hot." So hot, in fact, her whole body swarmed with fire ants at the thought.

"Huh," Jasmine said. Did the fact that this was the second time she had said *huh* mean that her friend was dumbstruck by her choice of boyfriend? If so, maybe this wasn't such a mistake after all.

"You guys have an interesting…" Jazz twisted her ponytail around her finger as she considered how to finish her sentence. Instead of finishing, she opted to change the subject. "How long have you been together?"

"Oh," Ashley said, swiping her hand across her lips, intent on removing any lingering bit of Colton Cross from her mouth. "Not long." Only the understatement of the century. "I doubt it'll last."

Beth snorted.

"Why do you say that?" Jazz asked.

Ashley turned to pour some drinks. Over her shoulder she said, "We're too different."

"How so?"

She shrugged. "We want different things. We have different philosophies on life. You know, the kind of thing that makes a long-term relationship impossible."

For the first time that evening, Jasmine's bubble of happiness wavered. She blinked at Ashley, a serious expression stealing over her features as Ash slid filled glasses to Jazz. "So then…" Her friend passed the pints of draft to the patrons waiting. "Why?"

Sticking her head between them, Beth answered for Ash. "Because the sex is so damn hot, she can't keep her hands off of him."

And for the millionth time, Ashley wished she was an only child.

Thankfully a rush of customers made it difficult to talk about the subject of her fake boyfriend anymore, and when the nachos were ready, fifteen minutes later, Ashley took them herself to the end of the bar where Colton was surrounded by his buddies.

"Here you go," she said, sliding the platter close before turning to go.

"Hold on a sec." He grabbed her wrist, holding her in place.

Ash's automatic response was to tug, but Colton was stupidly strong. "What?"

The sinful grin, that all the women in Half Moon were talking about, flashed across his face. "I'm of a mind to collect."

"Collect what?"

"A couple more kisses."

After a glance over her shoulder to see if Jasmine was watching—which she was—and then a glance over his to see if his friends were watching—which they were—Ash went up on tiptoes, placed her free hand on Colton's broad shoulder and whispered in his ear, "No."

This did not deter him. He released her hand only so he could slip his arm around her waist and pull her in tight against him. "If you were my real girlfriend, we'd be kissing right now," he said in a low voice, just for her. Then he waited to see what her response was to that.

She wedged a hand up between them, placing her palm flat against his chest—was it normal to have such hard muscles hiding behind a button-up shirt? No. She didn't think so—and pushed. There was no give whatsoever. "But I'm not your girlfriend. We're just pretending. Remember?"

"Oh, I remember. But you want to put on a show." With a tilt of his chin, he indicated Jasmine. "So let's put on a show."

"How'd you know?"

Using his knuckles beneath her chin, he tilted her head up. "There's only one reason a woman wants a fake boyfriend." He ducked down so that he was a mere inch away from her mouth. His warm breath made the wisps of hair that inevitably escaped the ponytail holder tickle her cheeks.

"What's that?" There was way too much breathiness in her whisper for her liking.

"To make her friends jealous." He waited a half second, his eyes glued to hers. When she didn't move, didn't shove, didn't object in any way, he lowered his mouth to hers and kissed her.

This was not the kiss she'd expected. She'd expected something for show, him bending her over the bar, making slurping noises as he pretended to make out with a passion he didn't feel.

That was not what this was. This was slow. Leisurely. Like he enjoyed getting to know her mouth. Like he wanted to explore her lips, the inside and outside of them. Not to mention deep inside her mouth. His big hand cupped the back of her head, and he tilted her—gently—one way and then the other, as he slanted his mouth over hers. When he finally pulled away, she was left, lips parted, panting.

"That ought to do it."

She blinked once, twice, three times before coming back to herself, suddenly cluing in to the fact that the whistles and catcalls were because of the show they'd put on.

Oh, shit.

What had she done?

"What the hell was that?" Colton's brother, Dillon, asked, giving him a dirty look.

"You're married. You should know what a kiss looks like."

Dillon arched a brow.

"Or, is that what happens once you knock 'em up? No more face sucking?"

With arms crossed over his chest, like he meant to intimidate him, Dillon said, "Don't be an ass. That was Beth Ozark's sister. The sweet one. Definitely not your type." He glanced over his shoulder, then indicated that direction with his chin. "Seems to me if you want a plaything, Brandi's more your speed."

Colton shifted to get a look at the other sister. Short skirt, tight top, nice hair, pouty lips. Their eyes met, and she gave him a dark, questioning look. Colton lifted his pint in salute.

And drank.

What was everyone's problem? So, he kissed a girl. Big fucking deal. It wasn't like he'd started it. He took another deep drink of his beer, finishing half, thinking about the kiss. The sister had tasted good. Fresh. Not fresh as in innocent, because she'd kissed him back like she'd done it plenty of times before. Done it, enjoyed it and meant to do it again.

He meant fresh, as in the way the grass smelled after a spring storm.

So why was everyone giving him a hard time?

"Nachos are on me," he said, indicating the platter with a wave of his glass. "Actually, the whole tab's on me."

"What's up with you?" Angus, a friend and rival bull rider from Billings, asked. "You worried you're going to lose in the ring this weekend and feel like making good on our bet early?"

"Naw," Colton said. "This is the last nice thing I do before I kick your scrawny ass this weekend."

A combination of laughter and groans followed by five hungry guys, demolishing a plate of chips, cheese, salsa and hot peppers. "But I'm cutting you off in a half hour. I don't need a bunch of sorry-assed, hung-over rodeo clowns blaming your shitty rides on me tomorrow."

"You talk big. Too bad it's all coming out of your ass."

Colton grabbed the last bunch of chips off the plate just before Rider, a calf roper from Butte, had a chance. "Sorry," Colton said with a smile. "Too slow. Hope that's not shades of things to come."

"Ahem."

He shoved the whole handful in his mouth and chomped. "Um...excuse me."

The guys around him grew quiet, their knowing smiles making him turn. Ashley was standing behind him, a very serious expression on her face.

"Can I talk to you for a sec?"

He removed his hat and ran a hand through his hair. "Sure."

Her eyes roved from his face to the faces of the men behind him. "Not here." Angling her head toward the back exit, she said, "Outside. If you don't mind."

"I don't mind one bit, darlin'." Draping his arm across her shoulders, which caused her to stiffen, he maneuvered them through the crowd to the back door, opening it so she could pass through first. On the other side of the door was a couple groups of smokers, leaning up against the side of the building, looking up as they passed, but not paying much attention to them.

"Over here." Tugging on his sleeve, she pulled him toward the alley and the quiet side of the building, out of earshot.

"You angling for another kiss?" he asked once she'd stopped and turned to face him.

She scowled. "No."

He stepped closer. "You want something else?" She was tiny, seemed even smaller looking up at him in the dark. "Something more?"

She shook her head hard. "Of course not."

He took another step, moving her until she was backed right up against the brick of the building. Colton didn't know why he did it, exactly. Probably because he was enjoying making her mad. "Then what are we doing here, sweetheart?"

If making her mad was his reason for lording his size

over her, his action had the desired effect. She threw her head back in exasperation and gave him a shove. "Oh, my God. You've got to stop calling me that."

"Sweetheart?"

"Yes. I'm *not* your sweetheart."

He propped a hand on the wall above her head and leaned. "But I thought you wanted to be my sweetheart. Just for tonight."

She wet her lips and his gaze dropped. While she may not be a beauty queen, Ashley sure as hell had nice lips. Particularly in the dim light where her tongue had left a bit of a sheen after licking.

"About that…"

"Uh-huh?" He forced his gaze up from her mouth.

"Um…"

Except then she started chewing on her lip and his gaze dropped right back down.

"C'mon. Spill."

"You know how I asked for just tonight?"

"Yep." God, he wanted to touch her lips. Why? He couldn't say.

"Well…"

Now those little lips parted, and she was breathing through them. He could feel her little pants against his cheek.

"See, I'm around all weekend. And, *you're* around all weekend."

"Let me guess," he said, propping his other hand on the wall, leaning in. "And your friend's around all weekend. That about sum it up?"

"Mmm-hmm."

"So…you want me to pretend to be your boyfriend for the whole weekend, is that it?"

She blinked rapidly a few times. "Maybe."

Colton smiled. He couldn't help it. The woman was

a weird combination of pissed off, turned on and a little scared all at the same time. The confusion flitted right across her ordinary features. Which was satisfying in a degenerate sort of way.

As much as he was enjoying himself, he wasn't a complete jackass. He eased back a smidge. "So, you want to hire me? Is that it? Like a cowboy gigolo?"

"Yes...no," she quickly corrected. "I'm just asking if you'll do it." She paused to swallow. "You know. Pretend we're together. That's all."

"So, pretend, huh? What exactly does that mean?"

"Well, I'll be at the rodeo and fairgrounds tomorrow, taking pictures. So, if I run into you, you act like my boyfriend."

"Uh-huh."

She waved a flustered hand between them. "And we don't have to do any more kissing, if you don't want."

Colton rubbed his jaw. "Seems like the kissing part is one of the perks."

"Okay, well..." She shrugged. "A little, then." She cleared her throat. "And then tomorrow night, I'll be here again, so if you happen to be here, same thing."

"Right. And then?"

She downright gnawed on her lip. "And then...there's the formal on Saturday night. I'm supposed to be there taking pictures. I assume you'll be there, too."

The truth was, he hadn't planned on going. He'd never gone to Half Moon High because his parents had moved after his and Dillon's oldest brother died. But Colton wasn't about to tell Ashley that. He had a warped need to hear where this was heading.

"Yeah, I'm going," he said.

"So...we go together. That's it. That'll be the end of it, I promise. We could even have a big blowup and break up by the end of the night." Her eyes lit up with a bit of fire and not of the angry kind. Like the thought of breaking up with him gave her pleasure.

Huh.

"So, you get what you want—a boyfriend. What do *I* get out of this?"

"I'll cover your pub tab for the weekend." A cringe flashed across her face...and then it was gone. Interesting. Colton considered her offer, but there was obviously something about it that bothered her. That was fine, he had other ideas, too. "I think the payment needs to suit the job, don't you?"

She got a cute little wrinkle in between her brows. "What do you mean?"

"I mean, the tab's fine for tonight. But what about tomorrow?"

"Umm...more beer?"

"I don't like to drink much when I'm competing."

"What then?"

Colton rubbed the back of his neck, and a slow smile inched across his face as he gazed down at her. "You have to do whatever I say."

"What? No."

"No?"

"Well, like what kinds of things?"

He leaned right in. "Haven't decided yet. But I'm sure I can think of something."

"Well, it can't be too crazy." She swallowed. "Or illegal."

"Don't worry. You'll like it, I promise."

Her eyes narrowed as she regarded him. She chewed on one side of her lower lip and then the other. "I don't know..."

"Hey." He stepped back, holding up his hands. "You're the one who needs the boyfriend. I don't need a girlfriend."

Don't want one, in fact, he almost said. "You don't like my terms? Find another stooge to play the part."

Taking a deep breath, she straightened her back, which brought the top of her head to right below his chin. God, she was just a little thing.

"You're right. Beggars can't be choosers. So, it looks like you're it."

Huh. That sounded suspiciously like an insult.

"I agree to your terms." She thrust her hand forward to shake.

He took it, and she pumped once before quickly releasing it. She pushed away from the wall and strode toward the back entrance without so much as a backward glance in his direction, as if she had complete control of this situation.

Colton grinned in the darkness because there was a certain amount of perverse pleasure to be found in playing this game with this woman. She thought she knew what was what. Well, he'd show her, and by the end of a pretend relationship with him, she wouldn't know what hit her.

3

THE BAR HAD finally cleared out, and the Ozark girls were busy cleaning up and counting receipts. Because of the two-hour time difference between Chicago and Montana, Jazz had faded around midnight, and Ashley had forced her to go up to her room at the hotel and go to bed. "We'll catch up tomorrow," she'd assured her before Jasmine left.

The back door banged, and Ash, Beth and the twins looked up. Brandi came striding in, her hair mussed, her lipstick smeared, an unrepentant look on her face.

"Where the hell have you been?" Beth asked, hands on her hips.

"Saying good-night to an old friend." Brandi dumped her apron on the bar, giving Beth a withering look from beneath her lash extensions. "Not that it's any of your business."

"We'd all like to get out of here tonight, so, yeah, it is my business."

"Seems to me that the one you should be worrying about is our precious youngest sister." Brandi narrowed her gaze at Ash, and Ashley's stomach cinched. She knew where this was going.

"What the hell are *you* doing with Colton Cross?"

"We've been seeing each other."

"Since when?"

"Since a while ago. We just—*I* just didn't want any-one to know."

"Why?"

"Because I'm not going to be here much longer, and I didn't think it was anyone's business and…"

"She's just using him for sex," Beth said, ever the help-ful older sister.

"You're sleeping with Colton Cross?" Zoe asked, glanc-ing at Chloe, asking silently whether she knew about this."

Before Ash could answer, Brandi spoke up. "As if *she's* having sex with *him*."

Ash propped her fists on her hips. "Of course I am."

"Right." Brandi stuck her elbows on the bar and leaned close. "Tell me about it."

Glancing from Brandi to the twins, then to Beth, Ash said, "No. It's none of your business."

Brandi shrugged and went back to counting her money. "Because you're not doing it. I can tell when someone's getting some. You—my uptight little sister—are not get-ting *any*."

"You're disgusting," Beth said. "Mom and Dad sure dropped the ball on the class gene when they had you."

Brandi ignored Beth—as usual—and poked Ash in the shoulder. "I don't know what you're up to, or why, but as far as I'm concerned, Colton Cross is still fair game."

"Oh, my God. You're jealous," Beth said, throwing her arms up in outrage. "You think you're the only one who can attract a man around here? Seriously, Brandi. Just be-cause Ash doesn't dress like a tramp, she's just as pretty as you. Plus, she's *way* nicer."

"Yep," Chloe concurred. "Way nicer."

Ashley appreciated the support, but what she really wanted to do right now was change the subject, finish cashing out and get home to bed.

"Oh, what a surprise. Everyone gang up on me and defend poor Ashley."

"You've just been outside with someone, doing who-the-hell-knows-what, and now you're moving in on Ashley's guy?" Beth shook her head, muttering obscenities beneath her breath.

The perpetual fights between her two older sisters was reason number 4,392 for why she *needed* to get out of Half Moon. Her family drove her bananas, and as long as she stayed, it would be high school *forever.*

Drumming her hands along the bar top, Ash said, "I'm done and I'm out of here." She grabbed her camera and purse from beneath the bar and waved to her bickering sisters. "Night, all."

"Get some rest," Beth called.

"Night, Ash," the twins called in unison.

"This isn't over," Brandi called after her.

Ash tilted her head toward the ceiling and whispered, "Mom, wherever you are? Your fourth child needs an ass whooping."

COLTON FINISHED UP the morning chores with the other ranch hand, Curtis, and then headed to the bunkhouse to shower before breakfast. He had taken over one half of the bunkhouse after the longtime ranch hand, Thaddeus Knight, had left. Turned out there was a lot more to old Thad than they knew, like he'd been hiding from the law for over ten years. Turned out he was innocent, and now he and his girlfriend were out east somewhere.

So Colton had offered to help out on the ranch on a temporary basis until they found someone more permanent. The Half Moon rodeo was always his first of the season before the rodeo season really got underway. He loved it. Different town every weekend. Riding, flirting, making a living doing the things he loved. Nothing to hold him or tie him down, just living in the moment every day of his life.

And this year was his year. This year he was aiming to qualify for the pro tour, which would mean competing professionally all year long.

After dressing, he made his way from the bunkhouse to the big guesthouse that his brother Dillon and his wife, Gloria, ran. It was already warm and it promised to be a perfect day for the rodeo.

"Where is everyone?" Colton asked as he sat down to a strangely empty dining room table. The guesthouse was fully booked for the weekend.

"Everyone went in to see the parade," Dillon said.

"Right. Why aren't you two there?"

"Too busy," Dillon said.

"Too pregnant," Gloria added, patting her belly. "What about you?"

"Parades aren't my thing," Colt said, filling his plate with bacon and eggs and helping himself to coffee. He turned to his brother. "Wish you were riding?" This would be the second year that his brother didn't ride in the rodeo, and it bothered him. Dillon had always been his idol, living the life of a rodeo cowboy.

But now?

Colton eyed his older brother from across the dining room table. He'd turned into their old man overnight. Giving up the excitement of the road to run a ranch. And seriously, the way he doted on Gloria, it was hard to watch. Finding any excuse to get his hands on his wife's growing belly.

His brother, the lone wolf Colton had always admired, had turned into a family man.

He never would have believed it.

"What time you heading in?" Dillon asked.

"Probably around noon. I'll help out with the stock."

"What time is your ride?"

"Three."

Dillon reached in his pocket and pulled out a set of keys. He tossed them across the table to his brother. "Use the trailer if you want. I cleaned it out last year, but the propane tanks are full. You can stay in it for the weekend if you like."

"Thanks. But don't you need help around here?"

"Nah. We'll be good." Dillon glanced at Gloria before asking, "You seeing Ashley today?"

Holy hell. He'd almost forgotten. He was supposed to be Plain Jane's boyfriend. "Yeah," he said dismissively. "I'll probably grab some lunch with her or something."

Gloria, glanced at her husband and then set her female sights on Colton.

Oh shit. He knew that look. Let the inquisition begin.

"Ashley Ozark? Isn't she the nice girl at Heart's Bouquet, the flower shop?"

Colton had no idea if she worked there. "You know her?"

"Sure," Gloria said. "She's been so helpful with the last couple of weddings we've hosted." She carefully set her mug of tea on the table. "So, where'd you two meet?"

"At the Prospectors." Colton dove into his breakfast.

"She doesn't seem your type."

With fork midway to his mouth, he said, "I wasn't aware I had a type."

Dillon and Gloria looked at one another and then simultaneously broke into laughter.

"Why isn't she my type?" Colton asked, not appreciating the laughter in the least.

"Um, she's an artist. A feminist. A smart girl with a future."

Okay. What the hell did people take him for? An idiot

who wasn't going anywhere? "You saying she's too good for me?"

Gloria pushed herself out of her chair, leading with her baby tummy. "I'm just saying that she doesn't seem like *fling* type material."

"Hold on, now," Dillon called after his wife as she made her way toward the kitchen. "Not to defend my depraved little brother, but it seems to me you tried to break up a fling last Christmas."

"Yeah, so?"

"So, you didn't call that one correctly."

Gloria may have waddled like a nearly full-term pregnant woman, but she could still spin around with the grace of a ballerina if the moment called for it. "What did you say?"

"I'm saying you were wrong the last time you tried to break up a fling."

She raised a single finger in the air and held it there, for effect.

Colton sat back in his chair, enjoying the show, glad the attention was off him.

"I was *not* wrong."

"Well, now…"

The finger was now pointed severely at her husband. "Jolie was not looking for a fling. Neither was Thad. Might I remind you, they are *still* together. By definition a fling would have ended long ago. Therefore, I was right."

"However you want to spin it, Red. You do that."

His fiery sister-in-law growled, right up until his brother stalked up to her, pulled her close and whispered loud enough for Colt to hear, "God, I love making you mad."

Colton blinked. Then he frowned. Then he shook his head.

Just because *he* liked making the Ozark woman mad didn't mean he had anything in common with his brother.

What he was doing with Ashley was a stunt. A game.

And if he also got a little turned on by making The Righteous Sister mad, it meant nothing at all.

ASHLEY WAS PLEASED with the pictures she'd gotten of the parade. She scrolled through them for the third time, the marching bands, the brightly colored floats. The cowboys. She enlarged a few, but Colton wasn't in any of them. After transferring her favorite images to a folder on her computer's desktop, she sat back in her chair and rubbed her stomach. It had been feeling funny all day. Probably something she ate.

The doorbell sounded, and she unplugged her camera from her computer and went to the door. Jasmine was standing there, wearing a cute Western-style top that sat low on her shoulders and a denim skirt. Instead of the customary cowboy boots everyone else would be wearing, she was wearing sandals, showing off her professional pedicure.

"You ready?"

"Sure. C'mon in while I grab my stuff."

Jasmine followed her through her father's house to her bedroom.

"Seriously," Jasmine said. "Your room is exactly the same. God, I wish my parents had stayed here in Half Moon. Their place in Denver just doesn't feel like home when I go there."

After graduating from college last year, Ash had come back to live with her father. It only made sense while she saved up money to leave again. Glancing around the room she'd grown up in, she now saw it through Jasmine's eyes. While she hadn't bothered to change it because she told herself she wasn't staying long enough to go to the trouble, she now decided it wouldn't hurt to replace the posters on the wall with some of her own work. Maybe repaint, too. In fact, she'd stop by the thrift shop on Main and see if she could find a few new-to-her accents to spruce the place up a bit.

Draping her camera bag over her shoulder, she caught a glimpse of herself and Jasmine in the full-length mirror beside her door. Jasmine looking sophisticated and mature. Ashley? Well, she fit in perfectly with her old bedroom: looking like she was *exactly* the same girl she'd been in high school.

"Maybe I'll change," she said on a whim.

"Do you want help picking something out?" Jazz asked eagerly.

Ash opened her closet and sighed. "If you want. There aren't a lot of options, though."

Rifling through the limited clothes in Ashley's closet, Jasmine picked out a checked top and an old pair of jeans. The choices weren't much better than what Ashley was currently wearing, and she said so.

"Do you have scissors?"

"Yeah, why?"

"These just need a few alterations." After Ashley passed Jazz the scissors from her desk, Jasmine quickly cut the arms off the shirt and handed it to her. "Put this on." While Ash buttoned up the shirt, Jazz went to work, chopping the legs off the jeans. It happened so quick, Ash didn't have a chance to stop her and tell her those were her second favorite pair.

"Now these."

Ashley wriggled out of the jeans she was wearing and slid the shorts up her legs. She checked her image in the mirror. She looked ridiculous. The shirt hung over the too-short shorts, making it look like she wasn't wearing anything underneath. "I think they're too short and the—"

"I'm not done." Jasmine interrupted. Using her manicured nails, she distressed the bottom of the shorts, created a fringe of denim. "You have amazing legs. You need to show them off."

"I don't know," Ash said hesitantly, thinking the shorts were something Brandi would be more likely to wear.

"The shorts aren't too short. The shirt is too long."

Snip. Snip.

Before Ash could stop her, Jasmine had begun to chop off the bottom of the shirt. Once she was done, she removed all buttons from her navel down.

"Now, we just tie this in front like this." She tied the two ends of material and turned Ashley toward the mirror. "Look at your stomach. People would kill to have a flat stomach like yours." Jasmine smiled at their reflections. "I think this is exactly the kind of outfit that Colton would like, don't you?"

"Do you think?"

"Uh, yeah. Watching him last night? He seems like a... manly man, you know?"

No, Ash did not know. Though a flashback from when Colton backed her up against the outside of the hotel made her catch her breath and warmed her skin. He'd certainly seemed *manly* then.

Jasmine reached around and unbuttoned another button so that the top of Ashley's bra was visible. "He's the kind of man that appreciates it when a woman looks like a woman." She grinned. "And this should do it."

Ashley gazed at her reflection. Did she want to tempt a guy like Colton?

Her sister's snide remark rang between her ears: *What the hell are you doing with Colton Cross?... I can tell when someone's getting some. You—my uptight little sister—are not getting any.*

Who said she wanted anything from Colton Cross? She didn't. But was there anything wrong with wanting peo-

ple to think that she *could* tempt a cocky bull rider like
Colton Cross?

Nope. Nothing wrong at all.

With shoulders back, Ash led the way to the front door.

Time to find the cowboy and enact a little simulated
seduction.

However, once she and Jasmine arrived at the fairgrounds, Ashley forgot all about Colton. Or, nearly. He
was like a morning coffee, long gone but the flavor still
subtly lingering hours later.

She was too busy taking pictures of the grounds, the
vendors, the contestants, the kids and games and food
booths, while listening to Jasmine catch her up on the last
five years of her life.

"I worked for a few years in my uncle's law firm. It
was okay, mostly administrative stuff. But I kept taking
classes in the evenings."

Ash focused the lens, zoomed in and focused again. A
child's face, crumpled, about to cry as his balloon slipped
out of his fingers.

Click.

"What kind of classes?" Ash asked, letting the camera dangle from around her neck as they wandered past
the chili tasting booths. "Law? You thinking about law
school?"

Jasmine snorted. "No. I'm not you." She sniffed. "Aes-
thetics. Hair. Laser. Makeup. You know. Beauty school
stuff."

Ashley glanced sideways at her friend. Jasmine had
never got the kind of marks that she had in high school.
But she was smart; she'd just spent more time on her wardrobe than on her studies. "You could be a lawyer if you
wanted, you know."

"Doesn't matter. I don't need to work."

Ash stopped and looked at her friend. "Why not?"

A weird smile crossed Jazz's face. "Parker's loaded. You should see our place in Chicago." She grabbed Ash's hands. "In fact, you should come visit. No. You *have* to come. You're going to be my maid of honor."

Typical. Jasmine hadn't asked Ash. She'd just decided. Ash both resented and envied that in her friend.

"So, tell me about Parker."

"Oh, you have to meet him. He's so…suave. Elegant. You know? He's like Mr. *GQ*. Or something."

Ash used the camera as a means to tune out her friend and her recitation of her perfect life. She wanted to be happy for her, she really, really did. But sometimes it was just so hard when Ashley's own life felt so insignificant and provincial beside her friend's.

Holding the camera in front of her face, she stopped just outside the rodeo grounds, taking a picture of four cowboys heading through the gates: three black hats, one white, Western shirts, bowlegged gaits, their worn jeans fitting perfectly.

Say what you want about cowboys, but rodeo boys had seriously nice asses.

Click.

"Excuse me, have you seen a little boy? Four years old, blond hair, Superman shirt, green balloon?"

Ashley lowered her camera. A woman she didn't recognize stood there with a baby in her arms and a worried expression on her face.

"I don't think so. What's his name?" Jasmine asked.

"Noah."

Ashley scrolled through the images on her camera, finding the one with the child and the balloon. Sure enough, the boy was wearing a Superman shirt. She showed it to the woman.

"Yes. That's him. Where was he?"

"Over by the ring toss. Maybe ten, fifteen minutes ago."

"Thank you." The woman hurried off.

Ash checked her watch. The opening ceremony for the rodeo would be starting in five minutes. She was supposed to get pictures. She hesitated. "Maybe we should go give her a hand."

"I'll go," Jasmine offered. "You go on in. I'll meet up with you later."

"Thanks, Jazz."

Jazz took off after the young mom, walking briskly to catch up. A stingy something-or-other reverberated inside Ashley's chest. How was it possible to both like someone *so* much but also resent them, too? Jasmine was her best friend, and Ash—well, she just had to say it—she was jealous of her. Thoroughly, bitterly jealous.

Always had been.

With a shake of her head, she entered the rodeo grounds, showing her press pass to the ticket takers at the door. *And what does she do about her juvenile jealousy? Does she own up to it? Oh, no. She goes and makes up a boyfriend to deal with it. Stupid.*

"Ash, up here."

As the chair of the Fair Committee, her father was sitting on the stage behind the announcer's podium. Ash climbed up to join him.

"This'll be the best spot for the opening ceremonies." He checked his watch. "You were cutting it close. It's starting right away."

"Then I'd say I was just on time." She took a quick pic of her father and the other board members, all wearing white hats. Then got a picture of the announcer, Hal Roberts, just as he welcomed everyone to the kickoff of the rodeo.

The opening procession commenced with the flag bearers on horseback, carrying the county, state and American flags. The rodeo princesses followed, then judges and competitors until the ring was filled with people on horses, stomping impatiently, picking up on the nerves of the competitors.

Before the national anthem could begin, there was a commotion just below the announcer's table.

Shit!

A little boy wearing a Superman shirt had slipped between the bars separating the ring from the stands and was now walking among the legs of the already nervous horses. His face was red, and he was crying loudly.

Hal's voice rose in a panic. "There's a young child in the ring. Can everyone please remain—"

Before he could finish, a cowboy slid down from his horse, jogged over to the kid and scooped him up. He carried him toward the stage and handed him over to Hal, saying, "You're okay, kid. Everything's fine."

That's when Ashley realized two things.

First, she'd been on automatic pilot, watching the entire thing unfold from behind the lens of her camera, capturing the scene, frame by frame.

Secondly, and more importantly, it had been Colton Cross who'd jumped down to save the kid.

4

WHILE THE COMMOTION settled down after the boy's panicky mother hurried onstage to collect her son, Colton glanced up to find Ashley Ozark—his pseudo girlfriend—staring at him, her camera pulled close to her chest like she was protecting it from stampeding hooves. He beckoned her closer.

Hesitantly, she moved forward, hunkering down at the front of the stage. "Yes?"

He grabbed the front of her shirt and pulled her in for a kiss. Possessing her mouth. The little gasp she made was rather satisfying, he had to admit.

"What was that for?" she whispered breathlessly.

His gaze flicked to the left side of the stage, where her friend was watching. "Just putting on a show, as commanded."

"Is that what all of this was?" She indicated the ring and the crying child with a sweep of her hand. "A show?"

Colton frowned. "No. The kid was about to be trampled, that was instinct. The kiss was for show." Though he'd be a liar if he said there wasn't a certain amount of instinct involved in wanting to kiss the uptight Ozark sister, as well. Though she was looking a little less uptight in her short shorts and tiny top.

"Okay." She pulled back, smiling awkwardly. "That should do it."

"Really? See, I'm not so sure."

"What do you—"

He yanked her down for another kiss. It was fun shutting her up with kisses. Partly because he wanted to teach her a lesson for thinking she had control of him, but mostly because the second their lips met, hers gave in: softening right up and parting for his tongue. Her lips meshed with his in a deliciously juicy way.

"Okay, okay," she panted against his mouth.

Colton grinned.

This time he let her pull away. She stood, crossing her arms in front of her belly, which was too bad because the little shirt she was wearing showed off her tummy, all nice and trim with the cutest little belly button. He wouldn't mind tracing that sweet little navel with his tongue later...

Whoa. Where had that come from?

"What time is your ride?"

"Three."

"Good luck."

"Thanks." Colton rubbed the back of his head. Maybe he was taking this fake boyfriend thing too far. "You gonna watch?"

She raised the camera. "I'm paid to watch."

"What time are you done?"

"Five."

"Okay. Meet me by the gate to the stockyard at five-fifteen." He stretched his back. "Then you can show me how much you appreciate me."

Her gaze narrowed.

He saluted. "Later, babe." Colton said the last part extra loud so that the friend would hear.

There. He'd done his part. Now he could go concentrate on his ride. Later he'd see if the Ozark girl would make good on her end of the bargain.

OF ALL THE harebrained schemes, this one had to be the worst. Colton Cross had just made sure everyone in Half

Moon Creek saw them making out. At the announcer's stage, no less. And he'd done it after heroically saving a kid from being trampled by horses. Though whether he'd done it to be a good man or whether he'd done it to make himself look good, Ashley couldn't decide.

Probably the latter.

"Thank God for Colton," Jasmine said from behind her.

Ash didn't turn. Instead, she watched as Colton leisurely jogged back to his horse. He grabbed the reins before gracefully swinging up onto the animal's back, and as he rode past, he tipped his hat to her.

Heat climbed from the pit of her stomach and up her throat. A fake boyfriend was not supposed to have such an effect on her. She stumbled to her seat beside her father and sat down, pretending to fiddle with her camera.

"So, you and Cross?" he asked gruffly.

She mumbled something that was somewhat of an assertion.

"You could do worse."

Out of the corner of her eyes, she snuck a glance at her father. Was it possible he was actually in favor of a relationship with Colton?

Nah.

The opening ceremonies came to a close, and the first event—barrel racing—began. Ashley turned her attention from Colton and focused on the task at hand, capturing as many images as she could. Time operated on a different wavelength when she was behind the camera, so she was barely aware of the fact that Jasmine had stayed as long as she had, watching the show.

When there was a break between events, Jasmine explained—with a knowing smirk—that she wanted to see the riding events, the bull riding in particular. Just the mention of it brought Colton to mind and had Ashley's stomach in knots because, well...

She wasn't exactly sure why.

It was probably the unknown payment for services rendered.

The man had gone above and beyond to act like her boyfriend. What exactly would he expect for it?

Time both seemed to inch by and simultaneously move at warp speed, and before Ash knew it, the bull-riding event was next on the schedule. Colt was the fifth rider, and the queasiness in her stomach intensified, culminating in a nauseous feeling when Hal called Colton's name as the next contestant.

He's just like all the rest. Just take pictures like he's everyone else.

Bolstering herself with a deep breath, Ash focused on the gate, snapping shots of the cowboy in question as he wrapped the rope around his right hand in preparation for the ride. The bull he sat astride was a massive yellowish beast, so ready to buck it was slamming against the gate before it even opened.

The horn sounded. The gate opened. The bull took off, jumping and spinning, kicking and bucking in a way that was completely unnatural for an animal its size.

Click. Click. Click.

Ash followed the movement of man and beast as they danced violently around the ring for what seemed like an eternity.

The eight-second horn blew, an outrider rode up, divesting the animal of the flank strap, and Colton hopped off. Even without the strap, the bull was angry, and seeing Colton in the ring—the man who'd been foolish enough to try to ride him—enraged the bull even more. At least, that's what it looked like to Ash. Her thoughts were confirmed when the thing charged, and Colton ran for the gate.

The audience gave out a collective gasp as Colton narrowly avoided the bull's horns before climbing the rungs of the gate to safety. Together, the rodeo clown and out-riders corralled the bull back to the stockyard, resulting in a cheer from the crowd and a hat wave from Colton.

"My, my," Jazz whispered in her ear. "That man must get your juices flowing."

Ash turned to her friend. "Colton knows how to put on a show."

"Yeah." Jasmine's eyes were aglow with admiration. "He's something else."

Really?

So now Jazz was seduced by Colton's manly displays? Because that was what it was, right? A display. An egotisti-cal need for attention. Why else would someone willingly climb on to the back of an angry animal and risk their life for all and sundry to witness?

"Listen," Jazz said. "I know you've got to stick around and take pictures, and I overheard you've got plans with Colton, so I'm going to head back to the fairgrounds and visit with some people. Catch up at the saloon tonight?"

"Yeah. Sure."

Jasmine reached for her hands and squeezed. "You are one lucky girl."

"Thanks," Ash said softly.

Lucky? Ashley didn't feel lucky.

More like one of the calves in the roping contest. In way over her head and about to be taken down and hu-miliated for all to see.

ASHLEY LEANED AGAINST the gate, wishing she hadn't cut off her jeans so that she could wipe her damp palms down the front. She gave herself a mental shake. This was stu-pid. Why did she feel nervous?

Because you have no idea what Colton wants from you.

True.

So, what would it be? A challenge? A dare? Something menial? Something sexual...?

Her tummy tightened at the thought.

And not in a bad way.

Shit!

"Heya, Ashley."

Ash spun around. Colton was there with the sun at his back, his hat pulled low so that his face was left in shadow.

"Colton." She cleared her throat. "Good ride today."

"Thanks. Ol' Yeller was sufficiently ornery."

"That the bull?"

"Yep. That was a lucky draw on my part."

"Why's that?"

"The tougher the bull, the higher the score if you make it to eight."

Ashley nodded. Being one of five sisters who lived in town meant she really didn't know all that much about the rules of the rodeo.

"So, what do I owe you for that overt display of affection by the announcer's stage?"

"Wow. Right down to business, huh?" He pushed his hat back, so she could see his face. His eyes sparkled irreverently.

Good God.

"It's a busy weekend." Ash indicated her camera. "So the quicker we figure it out, the quicker I can get back to work."

Colton's lips twisted. "All right. Show me your hands."

"Huh?"

He reached halfway across, holding his hands palms up. "Let's see them."

Hesitantly, Ash placed her hands in his. She was amazed by how small they looked. He rubbed his thumbs over her knuckles and then turned them over, palms up.

"They're nice. Are you strong?"

Snatching her hands away, she formed a fist and punched him on the shoulder. It was total instinct, and it took her a moment to realize what she'd done.

He chuckled. "Nice jab. Okay, let's go." He held his hand out as if to shake. "Take my hand."

"Why?"

"Thumb war, darlin'."

"What? You mean, if I beat you in a thumb war, we're square?"

"No," he scoffed. "It's a test. You ready? Set…"

"What kind of—"

He didn't let her finish. Before saying "go," Colton twisted her hand, captured her thumb with his and pinned it down.

"You cheated."

"So?"

She squinted up at him, her thumb still trapped beneath his. "One more."

"Fine." He released her thumb but still held her hand in ready position, though his pinky finger tickled the inside of her wrist, distracting her. "Ready…"

"Go." She dodged his big thumb with quick movements before managing to get on top of him. "Gotcha!"

So what if it was only for, like, a millisecond? She dropped his hand before he could slip out and beat her.

"Best of three," he said, his voice low, though his dark eyes twinkled dangerously.

The third time was an all-out battle, not just between hands and thumbs but their whole bodies. Ash tried to block him with her back so he couldn't see what he was doing, which only resulted in him tripping her—gently—and lowering her to the grass.

"What the…"

He settled his weight on top of her, holding her hand above her head, continuing to wrestle with her thumb while she attempted—unsuccessfully—to wrestle him off her body. What she did manage to do, however, was experience the wonderful weight of Colton on top of her: his legs twining between hers, his pelvis flush with hers.

Wait.

What was that?

Was he aroused?

The idea that Colton Cross had a hard-on because he was wrestling with her had the opposite effect of what she would have thought. There was *not one* part of her that felt incensed. On the contrary, Ashley fought an instinctual need to grind her pelvis up into him. More, to spread her legs and let him settle that steely part of him right along the seam of her shorts. She was so taken by surprise by her body's response to his arousal, she forgot completely about what was happening between their hands.

"That does it."

Colton claimed his victory by slowly pushing himself to his feet and extending his hand to help her up.

Of course she ignored it. Dusting herself off, Ashley steadied her features, determined not to show how much she'd enjoyed the impromptu wrestling match.

"You going to tell me what that was all about?" she asked, hand propped on her hip, gaze avoiding his.

"I just needed to make sure you're strong enough."

"Strong enough for what?"

"You'll find out. Come on."

Colton strode toward the parking lot on the other side of the stockyard, forcing Ashley to run to keep up.

"Strong enough for what?" she repeated as she raced after him. "And where the hell are we going?" He wasn't going to make her ride a bull or something, was he?

No. Maybe a cow. That would be appropriately humiliating.

Colton didn't stop until he reached his Dodge Ram 4x4,

which Ashley knew was his by the sound of the doors being unlocked by a fob.

Turning, he waited for her, resting his fists on his hips. "See, after a ride, I'm always sore. I usually go to Lucy down at the clinic for a massage." Then he pushed his pelvis forward and stretched backwards, groaning as he straightened again. "But I figure I'll save myself a hundred bucks by letting you give me one instead."

"You want me to give you a what?" Ashley sputtered. She looked Colton up and down. Then up and down once more.

"You heard me. C'mon. Get in."

She shook her head. Oh, no. This would not be good. "I can't. I've got to be at work by seven."

"Plenty of time. It's just a massage. That's all."

Sure, but last time she'd given a massage to a man, that wasn't all. That was only the beginning.

AFTER HIS RIDE, Colton had gone to the trailer to see how well it was set up. He'd gotten the whole massage idea quite by accident. It was when Angus, one of the hands who helped out as an outrider, was rubbing down his horse's legs. It made him realize that he'd forgotten to book an appointment with Lucy. Quickly following that thought was the realization that Ms. Feisty in the short shorts owed him.

A + B = C.

Simple.

Then he'd come back to the trailer to see if it would work for said appointment. All he'd had to do was hook up the electrical outlet and the water hose, and she was good to go. He'd picked up a few groceries and some beer from the corner store down the block from where the trailer was parked on the end of Elm and then had come back to meet Ashley.

He'd had no intention of making this about anything other than a massage, until they started wrestling.

Goddamn.

She may be tiny, but she was strong, and feeling her writhe beneath him with those long, bare legs and that taut tummy? Well, fuck it all, he'd gotten the stiffest Johnson he could remember having in a long time.

"So, where are we going to do this?" She eyed the couch and the bunk near the front of the trailer.

There was a slide-out bedroom in the back, and Colton indicated that direction with a swing of his head. "Bedroom in the back." He'd already made the bed with clean sheets from the cupboard.

"Do you have any lotion or anything?"

Shit. He knew he'd forgotten something. Reaching overhead, he opened a cupboard searching for something. There was a bottle of olive oil and some coconut oil. He passed them to her.

"Do you want to taste like olives or coconut?"

"And who might be doing the tasting?"

Her eyes went large before quickly narrowing.

"Seeing as you're my girlfriend and all..."

"Cool it, Colton."

"I'm just teasing." He leaned over her and plucked a blade of grass out of her mussed hair, a reminder of the wrestling match.

Bam.

Just like that, blood pounded toward his cock.

What was wrong with him? It must be the ride. Adrenaline always made him horny. That had to be it.

He flicked the grass toward the sink and reached for the tub of coconut oil, unscrewed the top and sniffed.

"Is it still good?"

He passed it to her so she could do the same. Taking a deep breath, she closed her eyes and took another. When she looked up, there was a guilty expression on her face. What was that about? She passed the tub back to him. "It needs to be heated."

With a raised brow, he took it and popped it into the small microwave oven. "How long?"

"Not too long. Thirty seconds should do it."

He set the timer and then grinned at her. "You've done this before, I take it?"

"Of course. I'm not a prude, you know."

"Never said you were."

Thirty seconds felt like three hours as Ashley avoided his gaze while they waited. She looked at the ceiling, the floor, the table, her fingernails, anywhere but at him. Finally, the bell rang, and he pulled the tub out of the oven and passed it to her. The scent of coconut pervaded the small space, and if he wasn't mistaken, Ashley's eyes fluttered closed as she took in another deep breath.

Interesting.

He eased past her and headed toward the back of the trailer and the door to the bedroom. It was a decent size for a trailer: queen-size bed with cupboards overhead and a built-in wardrobe in the corner. Dillon had used it while traveling the circuit, and Colton could see how it would be more comfortable than staying in crummy hotel rooms, town after town.

"So, ah…" Ashley stood behind him, looking apprehensive.

"You get comfortable, I'll go change."

"Right."

"Good." He moved past her, grazing her bare arms as he went. Sure the room was a decent size—for a trailer— but still close quarters with a woman you barely knew.

Pausing by the door, he said, "Unless, of course, you care to help."

She shot him a cool look. "I'm good, thanks."

Colton didn't realize he was smiling until he got to the tiny bathroom and saw his reflection in the mirror. Scrubbing a hand across his jaw did not remove his grin. Ah, hell. So he enjoyed teasing the woman. It wasn't a crime to enjoy teasing the person who was using him as a gigolo. He was pretty sure in such situations teasing was mandatory.

After hanging his hat on the back of the door, Colton stripped out of his shirt and jeans, hesitating for only a second before stepping out of his boxers, too. If this was a legit massage—which it was—then he'd be going in naked, like always.

Wrapping the only towel in sight around his waist—a threadbare thing—Colton squeezed out of the bathroom and returned to the bedroom. Ashley was sitting primly on the edge of the bed, her hands folded in her lap, the tub of coconut oil open beside the bed.

Her gaze flicked to his midsection and then up to his face. A tiny muscle twitched beside her mouth. "This is not professional."

"What do you mean?"

Her gaze flicked down again.

Colton glanced at himself.

Jesus Christ.

The thin towel did nothing to hide his raging hard-on.

5

WHAT THE HELL? This was twice in the span of half an hour that Colton Cross had a ginormous erection. Maybe he was just *always* erect. Maybe he had the opposite complaint to erectile dysfunction. Erectile hyper function. Was that a thing?

She'd have to look it up later.

Whatever it was, Colton did not seem in the least bit embarrassed. Oh, no. He strode right on by, leading with his Willy Nelson, like he was a stud on the lookout for a ripe filly.

What an ass.

He sat on the edge of the bed and flopped down on to his back, spread-eagle, his towel coming loose, revealing his hip bone.

Ash stared. She couldn't help it. She may have even drooled a little.

She gave him a dirty look and said, "Flip over," in the most officious voice she could muster.

With a groan, Colton rolled on to his stomach, which wasn't much better because in the process of rolling, his towel got snagged—likely on his woody—and now she had a full-on view of his heinie.

His muscular, taut, drool-worthy heinie.

Ash took a slow breath in through her nose and gently let the air out through her mouth. He may be all aroused for no apparent reason, but that didn't mean she couldn't be professional about all of this. No matter how screwed up "all of this" was.

She could handle it. Really, she could.

"Is there anywhere you'd like me to focus?" Ash asked as she crawled up onto the bed beside him, the maneuver feeling not as professional as she would have liked because her eyes were glued to his ass.

"Pretty much everywhere. Don't know if you've ever tried to hang on to a bucking animal, but it jars *everything* up pretty good." He moved his head back and forth. "Neck muscles always get sore, too. Kind of like whiplash."

"Oh. Okay." She moved up closer and then, very tentatively, swung one leg over him so that she was straddling his waist.

She sat perched above him when she realized the coconut oil was way over on the little shelf beside the bed. Leaning across the expanse of muscles that made up Colton's back, Ash reached for the tub, her bare tummy coming in contact with his bare hand, sending instant goose bumps racing down the length of her arms.

"You okay?" he mumbled into the pillow when she finally managed to right herself again.

"Yep. Fine." Except she wasn't, the proof of which was her too-high voice.

One more calming breath was needed as she dribbled warm oil onto Colton's back.

Why did he have to choose coconut oil?

She *loved* the smell of coconut. It reminded her of a holiday fling she'd had—her one and only holiday fling. It was during spring break a few years ago. A beach resort. His name was Alejandro and he was studying at Berkley, an exchange student from Spain. It wasn't that Ash hadn't dated. She'd dated plenty—if a nine-month relationship counted as dating—but Alejandro was everything she dreamed of in a man. Romantic, intelligent, sexy as sin. On many a cold night, she relived those moonlit walks along the beach, the long, slow kisses, the sensual way he spread coconut-scented lotion on her body. How she returned the favor. The way that sensual touch led to delicious sex in an open-air hut with the wind blowing in off the ocean.

Ahh.

Colton moaned, then muttered, "You're really good."

"Oh. Um. Thanks." She should not be thinking sex-laden thoughts while massaging a naked man in his trailer.

She took one more deep breath to steady herself, except the warm scent of coconut filled her senses, and she sighed, her clit throbbing so badly she wanted nothing more than to lower herself on to Colton's ass and rock like a cat in heat.

CHRIST. WHO WOULD have guessed the plainest of the Ozark girls would be so good at this?

Colton immediately chided himself for such an unkind thought. Ashley might be the least pretty of all her sisters, but she certainly wasn't plain. In fact, now that he thought about it—and lying beneath her while she worked miracles with his muscles gave him ample time to think about her—he had to admit that she had gorgeous legs. They were long in relation to the rest of her. Shapely, too. She might not have big breasts, but they were the right size for her frame, and Colton was willing to bet they had cute, little pink nipples that stood high and erect, even when she was standing upright.

Her hands were strong and sensual as they worked the knots out of his shoulders and upper back, pressing on the sore spots in a painfully good way and kneading the stiff muscles into relaxation.

"Oh, right there," he groaned.

Her hands felt so damn good, particularly when she ran her thumbs along the muscles that lined his spine.

"Harder," he said into the pillow.

"Huh?"

"Can you go harder?"

"Um. Sure."

There. That was even better. She hit some tender spots in his lower back, making him grunt.

"You sure that's not too hard?"

"No. It's perfect."

"Okay."

She continued to work those muscles, one side and then the other, and Colton felt as if he'd died and gone to heaven.

"I don't get it," she said, breaking the silence.

"Don't get what?" he eventually replied.

"Why you feel the need to ride a bull. A bucking one at that."

"Dunno. Runs in the family, I guess." Even when he was a little kid and had watched his older brothers ride, all he'd felt was excitement and an incredible amount of impatience for the day he'd be allowed to ride.

"But you're so sore and stiff right now. It can't be good for you."

"Maybe, but you don't feel it when you're doing it."

"Really? What do you feel?"

Colton was going to say something trite, just to get her to stop talking so he could enjoy the massage in silence. But he paused and thought about the question for a second. "It's kind of hard to explain."

"Is it the thrill? The danger? The rush?"

"Yeah, it is those things, but…" Colton thought about it for another few seconds. "It's more like—I don't know, maybe this sounds stupid, but—for those eight seconds, I'm there. I mean, I can't think about anything else. I'm completely focused on what I'm doing and where I am and how it feels. Those eight seconds are a lifetime. And it's— I just like being in that space of complete concentration. With nothing to distract me. Not what's gonna happen tomorrow. Not the things I regret about yesterday. It's just me and that damn bull for eight, very long seconds."

He shifted beneath her, thinking about what he'd just said. It was the truth. Maybe the truest thing he'd ever told anyone.

It was a few minutes later that he realized Ashley's hands had stopped moving.

He lifted his head and said over his shoulder. "Sorry. I don't mean to sound like I'm talking out of my ass."

"No. Not at all." She cleared her throat. "It's just weird."

"If you've never done it, I guess it would sound weird."

"No. I mean, what you just described? That's exactly how I feel behind my camera. Time is different and I see the world differently. Like how it's supposed to be. I don't think, I just see and do and capture the moments that we forget because we're too busy worrying about other stuff."

He lifted his head and attempted to turn around. "So, you know what I'm talking about?"

"I guess I do."

Her hands started moving again, and he flopped back down as her thumbs began working the base of his spine.

"Is it sore here?"

"Yep."

"You're really tight."

She dribbled a bit more oil onto his skin and worked that area for a while before moving lower, digging her strong fingers into his hips and using the base of her palms to work the knots in his ass.

"Damn, girl. You could do this professionally. You're that good."

"Don't get too used to it, cowboy." She unexpectedly slapped his ass. "This is a one-time deal."

"You sure you don't need a boyfriend for a little longer?

I'm around for a few more weeks. I promise I'll make it worth your while."

"Oh? And how, pray tell, would you make it worth my while?" There was a playful tone in her voice that was unfamiliar.

It was that playfulness that prompted Colt to roll over onto his back. He was gentlemanly enough to make sure the little towel covered things—sort of. "All manner of ways."

His hands brushed her bare thighs where she knelt above him. Tentative. Questioning.

For a split second, there was passion in her face. He was certain of it because her cheeks were flushed, her eyes were bright and the right side of her mouth turned up with sexy promise. Plus, her gaze raked his body in a way that told him she liked what she saw.

Then her eyes met his, and in a flash, it was all gone.

She blinked. Her brows drew together. Then she was scrambling to get off him, as if she might catch some nasty plague if she stayed there any longer.

Without a word, she scurried to the little bathroom, and he heard the water running before she returned a few minutes later, drying her hands on the front of her shorts because he'd taken the only towel available.

She shifted in the doorway, as skittish as a new foal. "Look, Colton. I know we're just messing around. And, I know you were just kidding right then." She pointed to him—more specifically at his barely covered erection. "But, I think we need to keep this on the up-and-up."

He snorted.

"What?"

"In what world is pretending to have a boyfriend in any way 'on the up-and-up'?"

Her face clouded over, and she was once again the snippety girl from the bar. "I'm just saying, given the circumstances, we should create some clear boundaries about all of this. We don't need anyone to get hurt."

Colton sat up, making sure the towel stayed put. "Who, exactly, is going to get hurt? You?"

Her mouth hung open in shock as she pointed at herself and gasped with great exaggeration. "Me? Oh, no. *I'm* not going to get hurt. Uh-uh."

Colt pushed himself to his feet, securing the towel low on his hips. Then he took two strides, which brought him right up in front of her. "So, you think *I'm* the one who is going to get hurt if we take this fake relationship a little further than sloppy kisses?"

"I don't know," she sputtered. "Maybe."

"Really." He put a hand on the wall above her head and leaned close, just like he'd done the night before. "You think if we have sex, I'll find you so irresistible I won't be able to let you go, is that it?"

She squinted up at him. "Stranger things have happened."

He reached for her jaw, tracing the line with the back of his index finger. "You know what I think?"

Ashley didn't say a word. She simply swallowed hard as she shook her head.

"I think you're worried about what will happen if you get a taste of me. In fact—" he cupped her chin and ran his thumb across her lower lip "—I think you're already worried."

Her breath came fast, whether it was from anger or arousal or a combination of both, it was hard to tell.

"You've got some ego," she panted.

"Nope. It's not ego."

"Then what is it?"

He shifted his gaze from her lips to her eyes. "It's the truth." Then he leaned down and kissed her. Nice and hard.

Best part was, she kissed him right back.

WHY, WHY, WHY, why, why?

Why had she let Colton kiss her in the trailer? Why?

And worse…why had she kissed him back?

Oh, she knew why. It was a moment of weakness. Colton had lulled her with his incredibly hot body and then seduced her with his thoughtful explanation about why he rode bulls.

But it wasn't real. It was a trick, a trap, a sham.

She should never have fallen for it.

"Everything okay?" Beth asked as Ashley wiped the already clean bar top for the tenth time.

"Dandy," Ash said through clenched teeth. "Everything is just dandy."

Beth placed a comforting hand on her shoulder. "Trouble in paradise?" She smirked.

Ashley shook her head, tightening the apron strings around her waist. After leaving Colton's trailer—and by leaving, she meant running out of there like the place was on fire—Ashley had come straight to the Prospectors Saloon. She'd made herself some fries and gravy, which were still sitting in the kitchen getting cold because her stomach was in knots over what had just happened.

And what didn't happen.

Even now, there were mutinous parts of her body that not only *wished* something had happened while Colton lay naked beneath her, they wouldn't stop thinking about the possibility that it might *still* happen, if only Ashley would let it.

Stupid bits.

Her body was so consumed by thoughts of Colton, the idea of eating was not in the cards, even though she was starving.

For sex, some random part of her shouted.

Yes, some good, old-fashioned, kinky sex, some other part called.

Hay loft sex, shouted another.

Trailer sex! all the parts cried out in unison.

"Shut up," she muttered.

"What's that?"

"Nothing. Where's Brandi?" She glanced around. "More importantly—" Ash indicated the nearly empty bar with a sweep of her hand "—where are all the customers?"

"There's a talent show going on at the stage down at the fairgrounds. Plus, the beer garden is open until eight. People should start trickling in soon."

"And Brandi?"

"She's probably singing at the talent show."

"Right."

"Where's Jasmine?"

"My guess is she's down there, too. She'll be by later."

"You having a good visit?"

"Sure." As soon as the word came out of Ash's mouth, she could hear the false tone.

The way Beth narrowed her gaze meant she heard it, too. Damn, it would have been nice to have a brother or two.

"What's going on?"

Ash rolled her eyes. "Nothing."

"Ash?"

"Ugh. Okay. I love Jasmine, you know I do, but sometimes…"

"Sometimes it's hard to compete?"

"Yeah."

"Hence, the hot new boyfriend."

Ashley felt her face go red. She tugged at one of the fringes of her shorts. "Maybe."

Slinging her arm over her shoulder, Beth hugged Ash to her side. "Hey, don't worry. I get it. Your secret's safe with me." She squeezed. "But a word of warning." With an upward tilt of her chin, Beth indicated something on the far side of the room.

Ash turned to see what, or rather *who*, Beth was referring to.

Colton stood in the doorway, his hat pushed back and—thankfully—quite a few more articles of clothing covered his muscular physique.

Too bad, whispered her naughty bits.

"The hot ones are always hardest to get over, even if it is all for show."

"No need to worry."

"You sure?"

"Mmm-hmm."

It wasn't a lie. Not really. Ashley didn't like Colton. No matter that he had all these freakishly developed muscles across his chest and back, or that he had the nicest ass she'd ever seen, or that he had the ability to say something that didn't sound completely macho or sexist. Unfortunately, as he ambled across the room toward her, she realized that no matter what she thought of him *logically*, the rest of her was irrational and could only think of one thing.

Jumping him.

Stripping him.

Having her wicked way with him.

6

THEY WEREN'T EVEN really dating. Yet, Colton didn't like the way Ashley had left him at the trailer.

Left? More like bolted.

Why did he care? Maybe because women never ran from him. More often than not, they threw themselves at him. It wasn't ego, like Ashley claimed, it was the truth.

And for some reason he felt he needed to straighten things out, but he wasn't sure why. Not exactly.

As he made his way across the floor to the bar, he met Ashley's gaze. The result of her direct stare was an increase in pressure behind his fly.

There it was. The other reason. Something about this woman continually made him hard. He had to know why.

"Hey," he said, once he was within hearing distance.

"Hey." She flashed a fake smile.

He gestured toward the draft pulls. "Can I get a Beaverhead?"

"Yep."

While she poured the pint, he leaned against the bar, watching her, trying to decide what it was about her that affected him so much. Her hair was blond and just above the shoulders, he guessed. Hard to tell when she always pulled it back in a ponytail. Baby fine. He knew this from the little wisps that tickled him whenever he kissed her. Her face had a nice shape, with high cheekbones and well-formed lips. And she had a long neck, kind of like those long limbs of hers, though she wasn't very tall, so it must just be a proportion thing.

She was a nice-looking woman. Maybe not of the *knockout* variety he typically went for, but attractive in her own way. Still...

He was no closer to figuring out what, specifically, it was about her that got him all hot when she slid the cool glass toward him.

"I thought you didn't like to drink when you're competing," she said.

"I don't. But I'm not riding again until tomorrow afternoon so one or two won't hurt."

She nodded before glancing over her shoulder at her sister at the other end of the bar. "So, about tomorrow..."

Right down to business. That irked him, which was why Colton spoke up before she could finish. "That's why I'm here."

She blinked, and her cheeks bloomed with heat. "Are you backing out?"

Is that what she wanted? For him to bail? If so, he would have thought there'd have been relief in her voice. But she didn't sound relieved; she sounded disappointed.

Interesting.

"Oh, I'm going. I wanted to talk about payment." He reached over and traced a line down the top of her hand. He had to see if this really was all business for her or if she felt some of the physical shit that he was feeling, too.

She snatched her hand back. "Okay, but first we should exchange numbers. You know, in case we need to get in touch or something." Her hand played with the open collar of her shirt, drawing his eyes to the place where her light blue bra peeked out from behind the fabric.

Damn.

He wanted to see the rest of that bra. He wanted to know

if her breasts matched the image in his brain. He wanted to see if she was as well proportioned as the short shorts and tiny top suggested.

"So…can I get your number?" Her hand fluttered a moment longer by her neck before digging in her pocket to pull out her phone.

"Of course." Colton found his phone, tapped in his password and handed it to Ashley. "You add yours and I'll add mine."

Colt added his info into her contacts, typing in the words Best Boyfriend Ever in the last name section.

He grinned as he gave the phone back to her.

She shook her head at what he'd written. "Really?"

"What?" Colton said with mock innocence.

She sighed heavily. "Okay, so, what am I going to owe you this time?"

He rested an elbow on the bar and leaned close. "Seeing as you've seen me in the buff…"

She sucked air so rapidly into her lungs, she made a little squeaky sound.

"I think it's only fair that you return the favor."

She stared at him, blinking.

"So, I'm thinking that after the whole party scene, you come back to the trailer and take your clothes off for me." It took a ton of self-control to say it without a stupid grin on his face.

Her brows drew together, and she looked to one side like she was watching something playing out in her mind. "You're saying you want me to do a striptease?"

"I believe that's what it's called."

"Kind of like a *you showed me yours, now I show you mine* situation?"

"If you want to frame it that way."

"I—"

He didn't let her finish. "Those are my terms, Ashley.

You want me to play your boyfriend? You've got to give a little something in return." He was being a dick at the moment, Colton knew that, but he couldn't help it. This woman both aroused him and brought out the bastard in him, resulting in his need to provoke her.

Hence the spur-of-the-moment striptease suggestion. He wanted to push her, wanted to see her get all hot and angry again. Or better, maybe she'd get turned on and playful, like she'd been for a split second in the trailer. And pretty much whenever he kissed her.

Goddamn, there was a sensual side to her, and Colton was determined to uncover it. Literally. Plus, she owed him. If necessary, he would remind Ashley that she needed him, not the other way around.

If that made him a dick, so be it.

He waited for her to get mad and counter his offer with something else.

"Okay. I'll do it."

It was Colton's turn to take a step back.

"You will?"

"Don't sound so surprised."

"Can't help it. You did bolt an hour ago."

"I know."

He came forward and leaned on the bar. "Want to tell me why?"

"Nope."

"Can I guess?"

"You can try."

"You're a virgin."

"A virgin." She made a derisive sound at the back of her throat. "No."

"Well, you were acting like one."

"I'm not a virgin, Colton."

"Okay." He held up his hands in skeptical acceptance of her denial.

"But that doesn't mean I'm easy. I bolted because I'm not attracted to you."

"You kissed me like you're attracted to me."

"So, I like kissing. Sue me." Breaking his gaze, she focused on the bar, tracing her finger through a wet spot, making figure-eight patterns. "That's why I can take my clothes off in front of you and not be tempted to do anything else."

"Whatever you say, boss."

Instead of getting mad like he expected, she raised her eyes and smiled. Strangely, it was the same sort of sexy, secretive smile she'd given him in the trailer. "You think you're irresistible, don't you?"

He shrugged. "I think when two people have chemistry, they should see where it goes."

"You know what I think?"

"What?" He frowned. Was she purposefully repeating what he'd said in the trailer? She leaned her small frame across the bar; this time she traced the back of his hand with her damp finger.

"I think you're used to having women, whenever and however you want them."

"I've never had any complaints."

Like a blinking neon sign, her expression flashed, *you're a prick*.

Why did that make him want to be an even bigger prick?

"Here's the thing, *Colton*. I'm not like those women."

She had that right. Colton was learning that lesson again and again, every time he saw her.

"And I'm not having sex with you—"

"We'll see."

"You didn't let me finish."

He magnanimously gestured for her to complete her statement, and she beckoned for him to follow her to the end of the bar. After lifting the hinged top, she slipped past and met him on the other side, gazing up at him with a semi sexy, semi smug look. She placed one small hand on his chest and grabbed his belt buckle with the other. While gazing up into his eyes, she slid her hand down, covering his package.

There was no hiding his arousal.

And this woman was *definitely* no virgin, which was evident in the way she rubbed her small hand up and down his crotch.

Fuck it. He wanted to spin her around, pull down her little shorts and take her right up against the bar for all to see. That would sure give the town something to talk about, wouldn't it?

Of course he didn't do it, but it was all he could think about until she grabbed his shirt collar, pulled herself up onto her tiptoes and came at him like she was going to kiss him. He leaned down to meet her, but she turned her face at the last second and whispered, "The only way I'm having sex with you is if I decide I want to."

"You'll want to." He grabbed her chin and brought her back to face him so he could claim her lips.

She ducked out of his grasp, patting his chest. "I doubt it."

ASHLEY'S HEART HAD been pounding so hard during the interaction with Colton, she was sure he would hear it and call her bluff. But he didn't. Neither did he try to kiss her again. He'd simply downed his beer and left. Just like that.

God.

She'd felt so powerful, so feminine, so freakin' sexy when she'd bluffed her way through that little scene with Colton. It was strangely addictive.

And when you take your clothes off for him tomorrow, what then?

Ashley leaned against the bar, feeling light-headed all

of a sudden. It was a couple hours later, and even though the place was teeming with patrons now, she couldn't stop thinking about Colton.

Massaging his naked body.

The feel of his stiff cock beneath her hand.

The idea of taking her clothes off for him.

What then, indeed?

Speaking of clothes, Ashley realized that she had nothing to wear to the formal tomorrow. Shit! What was she going to do? Would she have time to shop in the morning before heading back out to the fairgrounds to take photos? Could she find something that was both sexy and easy to get in and out of? She had to consider that fact. Some zipper down her back would not be conducive to a sexy striptease.

"Hello? Earth to Ashley. Come in, Ashley." Jasmine stood on the other side of the bar, waving her hand in front of Ashley's face.

The sight of her friend brought the reality of her fake boyfriend ruse crashing down around her. For the millionth time, Ashley wished she hadn't randomly kissed Colton Cross in a crazed panic. If she was going to make up a boyfriend, she should have simply made him up completely. Some guy from college who would do and say everything she wanted him to, because he wasn't real.

Yeah, right, Ash. Seems like you're real/pretend boyfriend is much more fun. Kisses, massages, stripteases. Why, you might even get crazy-assed cowboy sex out of this deal.

Thankfully, Ash was able to ignore her inner commentator because Jasmine interrupted the flow. "Seriously, Ash. You're the hardest worker I know. When are you going to take a break?" Jasmine scanned the length of the bar. "And, where's Colton?"

Not only did Ash's heart rate go from sixty to one

hundred at the mention of his name, her stomach dropped. Then it grumbled, and she realized she still hadn't eaten. Instead of answering Jasmine's question about Colton, she asked, "You hungry?"

"Yeah. All I've had was mini donuts."

"Let's grab something from the kitchen."

"Sure."

With Brandi back behind the bar—after whining about having to work during the town's biggest party—Ash informed Beth she was going to take a short break to eat.

"Okay, but hurry back."

She stole a couple of burgers from the grill—much to the twins' chagrin—and added fries to the side of the plates before motioning with her head to the back room, where things were a little less frenetic and they could talk in peace.

"I need your help," Ash said after swallowing her first big bite.

"Mmm." For all of Jasmine's sophisticated appearance, she demolished the burger like a ravenous beast, speaking with her mouth still full. "You know I'm happy to help. Whatever it is."

"I need a dress."

"For?"

"The party tomorrow."

Jasmine threw her head back and laughed. "You are the same old Ashley. God. Leaving these big decisions to the last minute? Didn't you do the same thing for senior prom?"

Ash looked down at her plate. Resentment flared— blam!—out of nowhere. Not about the dress—she'd worn one of the twin's old dresses—her resentment was because of something else altogether. Would Jasmine remember what happened? She doubted it. All Jasmine would remember was the fact that she'd been the belle of the ball, as usual, getting all of the attention.

Jasmine Sweet, prom queen of Half Moon High.

She rubbed the memory away and said, "Would you come shopping with me tomorrow? There's only a couple of shops here that will have anything halfway decent but—"

"Nope." Jasmine interrupted. "I've got an even better idea."

"What's that?"

Jazz pointed to the plate and said, "Finish that up and come with me. I've got the perfect thing."

SATURDAY NIGHT, ASHLEY sat on the counter in the bathroom, wearing Jasmine's dress while her best friend applied makeup to Ashley's upturned face. To say there were butterflies in her stomach was an understatement. There was a beehive. An anthill. There was so much activity going on in there she could barely breathe.

It didn't help that she'd only seen Colton from a distance today. It was when he was in the ring. His bull was smaller, and he'd completed the eight-second ride with ease. She thought he might have glanced her way once or twice but couldn't be sure. When she'd focused her telephoto lens on him it may have accidentally dropped to his midsection so that she had about twenty faceless crotch shots on her memory card.

Had he been avoiding her? Maybe. But so what? At least he'd texted to tell her he'd pick her up at six.

After tonight, the whole sham of a relationship would be over, as per their agreement.

That's why you need to make the most of it. The man is probably as wild in bed as he is in the rodeo ring.

"Jesus," Ash whispered.

"What's that?" Jasmine held her face up. "No, wait. Don't speak. I'm almost done."

Ashley tried to relax her face while Jazz finished putting lipstick on her lips, praying she wouldn't end up looking like a rodeo clown.

"You ready?"

No.

"Ready as I'll ever be." She slid off the counter and let Jasmine slowly turn her around toward the mirror.

Ashley blinked and then blinked again.

A stranger stared back at her.

Her nondescript eyes were lined and shadowed, not clown-like, like she'd feared when Jasmine brought out her huge makeup kit, but bringing out the gold in her brown eyes, making them appear large and sultry. The nose that she'd always considered to be on the too-short, too-stubby side suddenly appeared longer and elegant. Her lips—which she'd secretly considered her best feature—weren't done up in some bright color—à la Brandi's palette—but in a soft natural hue that had a pleasant sheen to it, making her lips look plump and...kissable.

"Don't you like it?" Jasmine asked. "Because I think you look gorgeous."

"I..." She touched her hair. Normally fine and limp, Jasmine had added some of her own products and then used a hot iron to give it messy curls that made her hair look full and tousled.

Sexy.

She smiled at herself, tentatively. "Wow," she said finally. "You're a miracle worker."

Jasmine grinned as she hugged her from behind. "It's easy when the subject is already so pretty." She adjusted the tie at the back of Ashley's neck. "And I just knew this dress would look better on you than it does on me."

Ash was just about to say, *I doubt that*, when the doorbell rang.

"That must be Colton," Jasmine said. "You ready?"

No.

"Yes." She squared her shoulders, lifted her chin and said, "Let's go."

7

ASHLEY'S FRIEND ANSWERED the door with a smile. "Hi, Colton," she said. "C'mon in."

When he'd texted to let Ashley know he'd be there at six, she'd asked if he minded picking up both her and her friend, which of course he didn't. The move did make him wonder if she was afraid to be alone with him. Which she should be.

While he absolutely accepted that it was Ashley's choice whether they take this fake relationship all the way—for recreational purposes—Colton had decided he was going to make damn sure she made the right choice.

"How are you doing, Jasmine?" Colt bent and gave Jasmine a gentlemanly kiss on the cheek. The move had him breathing in her perfume, which was a little too strong for his liking. He preferred the way Ashley smelled, clean and fresh, like orange blossoms.

"I'm great, thanks, and I..."

He didn't hear another word that came out of her mouth. "Holy shit," he muttered.

Standing on the stairs behind Jasmine was a *knockout*. No, better than a knockout, she was something that could have walked straight off the cover of one of those magazines by the grocery checkout.

She was...perfect.

Some soft luminescence radiated from within, making her look otherworldly.

Beautiful.

And that dress.

Fuck. That dress was sexy as hell. Sleeveless, it had two wide straps that just covered her chest, leaving an enticing gap between, and tied up around her neck, showing off some killer collarbones and slim arms. There was no possible way she was wearing a bra beneath a dress like that.

The skirt was short but not too short, poofing out a bit, accentuating her narrow waist and slender legs.

"Hi, Colton." Her voice was soft and smoky and so damn sexy.

The result was immediate.

His cock woke up, stiffening in blind anticipation of what might happen tonight.

Might?

Oh. no.

There was no *might* about it.

"You clean up well," Colton said with a rough edge around his voice.

Her expression faltered, and he realized that wasn't something a boyfriend would say. "I mean, you look... beautiful, babe."

Her lips turned up in a soft, faltering smile.

He didn't even have to remind himself of his role as he crossed the distance, slipped a hand around her waist—his fingers coming in contact with the soft bare skin of her lower back—and pulled her close. "You know," he whispered. "I'm not sure I can wait until later."

"For what?"

He drew a line up her backbone. "You know what."

She let him pull her body against his, and when he bent down to kiss her cheek, she turned her face, this time toward him, so that their lips met. The kiss was soft and full of promise.

Goddamn, he had to have this woman. Maybe that would cure him of this uncontrollable arousal. Colton took her hands and pressed his lips against her knuckles.

"You ready?"

She nodded.

He held her hand, as a good boyfriend would, and turned toward the door. Jasmine was there waiting, her eyes large and liquid. Five seconds in Ashley's presence and he'd forgotten all about Jasmine. Crazy.

"I must be the luckiest man in Half Moon tonight," he said, covering up his lapse in memory.

"Why's that?" Jasmine asked.

"I get to escort the two most beautiful women in town to the party. It doesn't get much better than that."

Ashley leaned close and whispered in his ear, "Don't overdo it." Then she stroked his cheek like she'd whispered something naughty and moved away to grab her camera bag.

He didn't reply until he'd walked the women out to his truck and opened the door to the extended cab, helping Jasmine into the backseat. Once the door was shut, he paused by the passenger door before opening it for Ashley.

"I'm not overdoing it."

"Yes, you are."

"Which part?"

She gave him a dirty look in reply.

"You don't think you look good?"

"Jasmine does, but..."

"Why do you do that?"

"Do what?"

"Put yourself down?"

"I don't. I'm just realistic. I know I don't compare to Jasmine. It's—"

He stopped her with a kiss. Against her mouth he said, "We may not be together for real, but I'd choose you over her any day." He touched her bottom lip with his tongue. "And I'm not overdoing it when I say I want you." With knuckles beneath her chin, he tilted her head up. "I want *you*, Ashley Ozark, so make sure you know what you want before you come over to the trailer tonight."

IT HAD TO be a lie, didn't it?

Colton Cross wanted her? Really?

Well, his cock certainly seems to.

Yes, but he was probably one of those guys who was so virile he was ready to go anytime, anywhere. It wasn't her, it was him and his overactive sex drive. However, through the entire meal she couldn't help sneaking peeks at the crotch of his dress pants to see if there was any indication of arousal.

Hmm. Hard to tell.

"Do you want to touch?"

"Excuse me?"

Colton carefully lifted her hair away from her ear and bent close. "You keep eyeing my fly, and I was just wondering if you wanted another touch. I wouldn't be opposed."

He took her hand and placed it on his thigh. Was he flexing it or was his leg really that muscular?

A blinding and sudden image of his toned body lying naked beneath her jolted her, making her hand twitch in an upward direction so that her pinky grazed the hard, swollen, male flesh beneath the fabric.

"You're killing me, you know that?" he whispered hotly against her cheek.

On the other side of her, Jasmine whispered, "Seriously, you two need to get a room."

Inhaling deeply and inadvertently catching a delicious

whiff of Colton's cologne—God, the man smelled edible—
Ash turned toward her friend who was pretending to scowl.
At least, she thought she was pretending.

"Sorry," Ash said. "Colton doesn't like to have sex when
he's riding which means he's a little backed up."

"I heard that," Colton said. He leaned across her to
speak directly to Jasmine. "It's a lie. Ashley's too busy
working this weekend, so she won't give me any. Can you
talk to her about that?"

She kicked him beneath the table.

"Ouch," he said exaggerating the offence. "She kicked
me."

Jasmine laughed at their antics, but if Ashley wasn't
mistaken, it was a forced sound, which was odd.

She was about to ask what was going on when the pro-
gram started, and Ashley excused herself from the table in
order to walk around the room to take pictures. As mayor
of Half Moon Creek, her father was the first to speak,
welcoming everyone back to town and going into some
history of the area and the school before handing the mic
over to one of the former principals. Ashley wove between
the tables, doing her best to be inconspicuous, taking candids of the guests whose ages ranged from octogenarians
to those who graduated a few years ago.

"Wow, Ashley, you look so beautiful," Sage, a local
shop owner, commented as she passed.

"Thanks," Ash said.

Beth stopped her next, "Where'd you get that dress?
It's super cute on you." She nudged her husband, Derek.
"Doesn't Ash look good?"

"Oh, yeah. Real pretty."

"It's Jasmine's," Ash explained.

Leaning way back in her chair so she could glance over
at Ashley's table, Beth gave her a lewd wink. "I bet your
boyfriend likes it."

Leslie, the owner of the flower shop where Ashley worked, also stopped her. "Look at you, you gorgeous thing."

Okay, so much for being inconspicuous. Ash squeezed between two tables and made her way to the outer edges of the gymnasium, taking photos as she went, only returning when the lights were dimmed for the slide show, telling the history of the school and town.

"Where's Jasmine?" Ash asked, noticing Jasmine's seat was empty.

"Someone called."

"Was it Parker?"

Colton shrugged.

Jasmine still hadn't returned when the slides from their graduating class came up. Out of the five slides, two included Jasmine, one of which was from prom. Jazz and Curtis Bellamy, dancing together after being crowned King and Queen.

The image triggered a memory followed closely by an unsettled squishy something in her stomach...

Jasmine reapplying lip gloss in the mirror after insisting Ashley accompany her to the bathroom.

"C'mon, Ash," Jasmine said after smacking her freshly glossed lips. "Who is he?"

"Who's who?"

"You know. The guy you've been watching all night."

"I don't know what you're talking about."

"C'mon. Is it Bret Evans? No? Simon Murphy?" She turned from the mirror to face Ashley, squinting at her. "Why won't you tell me?"

She remembered hesitating, but then thinking, if she couldn't tell her best friend, who could she tell? "Curtis," she'd said, still able to recall the blush creeping into her cheeks. "It's Curtis Bellamy."

Half an hour later, it wasn't Ashley dancing with Curtis, it was Jasmine.

"Why aren't you in any of those pictures?" Colton asked.

Because I'm invisible, Ashley thought to herself.

To Colton, however, she said, "Even back then, I took the pictures."

"Work, work, work, huh?"

She shook her head. "No. I just prefer to be behind the lens, that's all."

Colton watched her for a moment before lifting her hand from her lap and squeezing. It was the most natural thing in the world.

And yet, it wasn't. By the end of the night, she'd be breaking up with him, and then, stranger still, she'd be taking her clothes off for him, for payment.

God. She was practically prostituting herself for a lie.

So why did holding Colton's hand feel so good?

When Jasmine returned, Ash reluctantly pulled her hand from Colton's to turn to her friend. Jasmine's expression appeared serious and...upset?

"Is everything okay?" Ashley asked.

Jazz glanced up and plastered a smile on her face. "Yeah, fine."

"You just missed the pictures. There was one of you and Curtis."

"Curtis Bellamy?" A glow returned to Jasmine's eyes. She glanced around at the tables in their vicinity. "Is he here?"

"I haven't seen him."

"Too bad."

As far as Ashley knew, Curtis still worked for Colton's brother on their ranch. He'd always been the quiet, introverted type, which was probably why she'd been drawn to him in high school. Not that she had any feelings for him one way or the other anymore; after seeing him and Jasmine together that night she'd banished all romantic notions completely.

A twang of a guitar and random drumroll interrupted her thoughts. The band, a local group called the Haymakers, were warming up to start the dance portion of the evening, and Ashley realized that her fake relationship with Colton Cross would soon be coming to an end.

Jasmine nudged Ashley. "You two going to dance?"

"I should probably take some pictures first, maybe later."

Jasmine reached across Ashley and tapped Colton's forearm, "Do you want to help me get this party started?"

Colton glanced at Ashley, as if asking permission, which was weird because he could do whatever the hell he wanted.

"Do you mind?" Jazz asked her.

Ashley shook her head slowly. "Of course not." She watched them make their way to the dance floor, just as the band launched into their first song, and a tingling began at the base of her throat.

Ashley grabbed her camera and followed the two toward the dance floor where other couples were also congregating. There was no reason to feel upset. Jasmine was engaged. Colton wasn't Curtis, and this wasn't high school.

However, from the moment the music started, Colton spun Jasmine around in and out between the other dancers, creating a spectacle. She took a few pictures but was distracted by something hot and uncomfortable milling about in the pit of her stomach.

Ash focused the lens and depressed the shutter. However, viewing the dance through the lens was too familiar. Old resentment mixed with new, and an acrid cloud of bitterness surrounded her, filling her lungs like a poisonous gas and making it impossible to breathe. Had looking through the lens brought everything back? The fact that this was the very same gymnasium where Jazz had danced with Curtis right after her confession. The fact that, just like that night, she was on the sidelines, taking pictures, completely invisible.

While Jazz scooped her guy.

Not that Colton was *her guy.*

Slowly, she lowered the camera. Then she removed the strap from around her neck and returned to the table to put the camera in the bag. With her shoulders back, she strode out to the dance floor and tapped Jasmine on the shoulder. "Can I cut in?"

"Oh." Jasmine stopped mid-two-step. "Of course."

Ashley moved in front of Colton and extended her hand, which thankfully he took. "I hope you don't mind."

"Of course not." He smiled down at her.

She tried to take a step in time to the music, but he wasn't moving.

"You know I'm supposed to lead, right?"

"Of course."

"You sure? Because I get the feeling like you want to lead."

"I know how to dance, Colton," she growled, but not because she was upset. More because it was fun to bicker with him.

"Okay."

After a smug look, he tightened his grip on her and started to dance. Holy hell. Colton was a good dancer. No, scratch that. He was a *great* dancer; he held her lightly and yet directed her body with authority, moving her this way and that, spinning her so fast her little skirt flew up to dangerous heights.

It was marvelous and made her think of one thing only.

If Colton was this good on the dance floor, what the hell would he be like in bed?

DANCING WITH ASHLEY was like dancing with air. Most women had a hard time when he moved so quickly. Not Ashley. She moved as if she was an extension of his body; the slightest pressure on her waist or on her hand and she moved the way he wanted her. So he turned her faster, making her skirt spin out so high he was tempted to see what was underneath.

After the third song, she was laughing in a gasping out-of-breath way—which was adorable—but not quite as adorable as the way she collapsed against his chest after the song ended.

"Damn. That was fun."

"It was." She tilted her head to look up at him, her face flushed, her eyes full of life. How could he ever have thought she was plain?

She was anything but plain.

Without thinking, he cupped her jaw as he bent down to her level. "Here's hoping we have fun all night long."

He waited for her to tug away, but instead, she gazed up at him with that smile. The secretive one. Colton liked that smile. He liked it a whole helluva lot. There was promise in that smile, and he'd take promise over nothing at all.

"And remember—" she patted his chest "—I need to break up with you before the night is over."

Shit. He'd forgotten about that part. Seemed a shame, somehow. "Why do *you* have to break up with *me*?"

"If you break up with me, people will feel sorry for me." She feigned a pout. "Aww, poor Ashley. Always a bridesmaid, never a bride." Shaking her head, she said, "No, thank you."

"Is that what you think?"

"What?"

"That you're always overlooked?"

This time she threw her head back and laughed. "It's not what I think, it's what I know."

She said it so matter-of-factly it made Colton realize how very much she believed it. Worse, how he'd probably contributed to that set of beliefs.

"C'mon." She tugged his hand. "Let's go back to the table."

But the band had started playing a slow song, and he held her in place. "Let's dance one more."

A little wrinkle formed between her brows, but when he pulled her into his arms, she entered willingly. God, she felt good as he held her. Smelled good, too, citrusy and sweet. With Colton's one arm snug around her waist and the other hand on her bare back, Ashley had nowhere to put her hands except around his neck.

In heels, she came to just below his chin, and he had to admit, he liked the height advantage. He liked the way she had to look up at him. Liked the way her slight body swayed against his.

Really liked the press of her breasts against his chest.

"So, how should we do it?" she asked, nibbling on her lower lip.

"Well, after you take your clothes off, I'm thinking I'm going to lick you from your toes all the way up to your mouth and then head south again, settling somewhere in the middle."

She blinked, her fingernails digging into his shoulders. Wetting her lips, she said, "I mean the breakup."

"Oh, I'll leave that up to you. I'm too focused on the after-party."

"Is sex the only thing you think about?" If she meant to sound condescending, it didn't come off that way. It could have been because her hands slid from his shoulders, down his back and were now holding tight to his ass.

"Only when I'm around you." There was more truth to that statement than she would likely believe. But he didn't care. And if she thought she was allowed to get a handful of ass without reciprocation, then she hadn't learned anything about him yet.

Fair's fair.

8

THE HAND THAT had been resting on Ashley's bare back now slid down the flouncy fabric covering her butt. Despite all the material in the skirt, she could feel Colton's strong hand grasping her flesh through the springy underskirt of her dress.

God.

She itched for him to slide his hands right up under her skirt, to settle his palm over the satin of her panties, to pluck away the elastic circling her leg and move underneath. Touching her.

All she'd been able to think about, all day, was having sex with Colton. Tonight. Her one and only chance.

Oh, she'd played it cool at the bar last night, a magnificent performance, but seeing him in his suit, an appreciative gleam in his dark eyes, just enough stubble across his strong jaw to be stylish and sexy...where was the cocky cowboy now?

Colton was all cool sophistication, the kind of man who would catch her eye at a party—except she'd never have the nerve to approach someone like him.

Now, here she was, dancing with him—more like grinding with him—as if it was the most natural thing in the world. So strange.

"Hey," she said softly, tilting her head back to meet his gaze. "I was thinking..."

Colton's eyes were hooded, and his mouth appeared so warm and inviting and…close. She went up on tiptoes and kissed him.

One of his hands left her ass to tangle into the hair at the back of her head, and his other hand clutched her butt even tighter.

"I was thinking the very same thing," he whispered. "Let's go."

Ashley blinked up at him, her body still swaying to the country ballad, her hands roaming just as much as his were in a way that was barely decent for a dance floor.

Colton's nostrils flared as he drew a deep breath.

It was like he'd made a decision behind those half-shuttered lids because he removed her hand from his ass and tugged her toward their table, instructing her to gather their things.

She didn't object. Couldn't object because she seriously could not get out of there fast enough, and once she had her wrap, clutch and camera bag, she found herself dragged toward the exit doors.

However, when they were a few yards away from the door, Brandi stepped out of a crowd of people, stopping them.

"Hey, Brandi," Ashley said, still breathless from the dance, although she really shouldn't have been, considering the last one had been slow.

"Ash." Her sister's gaze flicked to Colton. "Where are you two going? Aren't you supposed to be taking pictures tonight?"

Shit.

Ashley tugged her hand from his, playing with the strap of her camera bag, feeling sheepish.

"Nope," came a voice from behind them. Ash turned. Jasmine was there, grinning. She unhooked the camera strap from Ashley's shoulder and slid it over her own arm.

"I'm taking pictures for the rest of the evening. Ashley hasn't had any time off, and if these two don't get some alone time, poor Colton is going to burst." She winked.

Ash smothered a laugh.

"That might be a slight exaggeration," Colton replied, though by the quirk of his month, he wasn't offended by her comment.

Brandi made a sort of humph sound before opening the door and making a show of ushering them through but not before Ashley hugged her friend, whispering, "Thanks," in Jasmine's ear.

"No problem," she replied. "Go have fun. You deserve it." She gave Colton a finger wave, to which he nodded in return.

"COME ON." HE TOOK Ashley's hand again, it was so small and warm and felt so good. He wondered how it'd feel wrapped around him. Touching him. Not like she'd touched him during the massage, but the way she'd been touching him out on the dance floor.

He didn't drop her hand again until he got to the truck, to open the door for her and help her up to her seat. Anything to hurry up this process.

"Thanks," she said softly.

Once he was behind the wheel, he turned to her, noticing how she was perched primly on the other side of the bench seat. "Come closer."

She didn't move. Instead, she said softly, "You didn't have to do that, you know."

"Do what?"

"You don't have to pretend when there's no one around to pretend for."

He hadn't started the truck yet, so the cab was dark, leaving Colton to guess the expression on Ashley's face, but her uncertain tone said it all.

"Come here."

Her silence dragged on too long, and Colton was done waiting. He slid over, reached across the empty space, wrapped his hand around her back and hauled her close.

"Hey," he said, brushing her shoulder. "If you don't want to do this, just say the word."

His fingers followed a delicate cord in her neck up to her jawline. From there he stroked her cheek, up over her cheekbone and down again to touch her lips.

Though it had all been quite unconscious, his touch softened the firm line of her mouth until it fell open as he made a second pass, her tongue darting out to lick his fingers. Sweet and sexy. That's what she was. Oh, and occasionally bossy and abrasive.

Colton leaned down, touching his lips to her open mouth, and, without warning, her hands came up around his neck, pulling him tight and kissing him.

Softly at first. Then...

Wildly.

Passionately.

Her mouth was hot and wet and tasted of red wine. She lifted herself up so she was half on his lap, her bare leg twining around his, and Colton finally found his way beneath that short skirt, stroking her hip and the lovely globe of her ass through her soft, satiny panties.

"What are we doing?" she asked, breathlessly against his mouth.

"My guess? We're not breaking up tonight." He licked across her lips while his fingers played with the elastic band of her panties.

"Shit!" She pulled back. "I totally forgot."

"Does it really matter?"

She hovered above him for a moment. "Maybe not." And then her hand was on his fly, rubbing just like she'd done in the bar.

He groaned. "Please, tell me you're not just teasing me," he whispered in her ear before tilting her head so he could suck on a sweet, tender spot just below her ear.

"I haven't decided yet." Her fingers curled around his belt, holding on tight.

"You are going to kill me, you know that?" Colton gazed up at this woman who was as unexpectedly exciting as she was passionate.

"Good."

He took her mouth, again. Hard.

She had to know how much he wanted her. All night he'd been able to think of little else besides getting Ashley alone. In the trailer. Seeing her for the first time. Touching her for the first time. Kissing her, tasting her skin.

How it would feel to slide himself right up inside of her, how it would feel to have her move and writhe beneath him like she'd done when they were wrestling.

Her kiss seemed to indicate she knew.

Oh, and the hand stroking his cheek? Surely that was an indication of her desire for him, too.

Then there was the hand that rubbed his cock through the material of his pants.

Yes, she knew. She had to know.

"Ash," he moaned, on the verge of unzipping himself and taking her right here in the high school parking lot.

She sucked in a deep breath and moved off him to sit beside him. Her head lolled against his shoulder while her hand lay covering his rock-hard erection.

"C'mon, cowboy. Let's go."

CRAZY-ASSED NERVES fired up inside Ashley as Colton fit the key into the lock and opened the door to the trailer. She'd been this close to giving the man a blow job in the truck. Seriously. That's how much she wanted him.

Colton Cross? The egocentric cowboy?

Yep.

Except that she didn't quite see him that way right now. Sure, his attentiveness was feigned, but could he pretend to be aroused? She didn't think so.

The trailer was quiet, with only the sound of the whir of the air conditioner, and Ashley reached along the wall to find a light switch, but Colton had other ideas.

He came up behind her, turned her into the circle of his arms and kissed her in the same feverish way he had in the truck.

Was it fake? Was it all for pretend?

Ashley stopped caring. It felt too good to dissect and analyze, particularly when his tongue searched her mouth with such thoroughness it took her breath away.

"Colton, I…"

"No more talking." He stopped kissing in order to shrug out of his suit jacket, which he tossed. He pulled her close to kiss her some more while he backed her up toward the other end of the trailer where the bedroom was. It wasn't until they were inside that he stopped kissing her in order to switch on a light beside the bed.

Then he approached, his gaze fierce, his intention clear. But he didn't ravish her again; he paused right in front of her, cupping her cheek and tilting her face up. "I know we had a deal. I know you were supposed to do something for me, as some sort of fucking payment, but I'm not going to lie, Ashley. I want more." He grazed her cheek. "I want to touch you, kiss you, undress you. I want to feel your skin right up against me." He brushed a thumb across her lips. "I want to be inside of you."

The words were so gruff, there had to be some truth there.

"So, I need to know, right here and now, before we do anything else, if that's what you want, too."

His thumb caressed her jaw while he waited for her to answer.

She knew her answer, had known it all day. But still she hesitated.

Colton frowned. "Otherwise I'll take you home…"

No.

"No," she said, turning her face into his hand and kissing his palm. "I want the same thing." She tilted her head back to gaze at him. His lids were lowered, his jaw tense, his nostrils flared. Ashley might not have understood his attraction to her, and neither did she totally understand her attraction to him, but it was there nevertheless.

"Thank God." Colton took her hands and pulled her toward the bed. Before sitting, he turned her around in his arms and gently untied the straps at the back of her neck. Her lids fluttered closed as the ties tickled her bare shoulders. It was exquisite, the brush of his fingers against her skin, the swish of the fabric, until finally he had both halves loose and let them slither down her shoulders, baring her chest.

"Turn around."

She turned.

He didn't touch, he only gazed at her breasts, making appreciative sounds at the back of his throat. After lowering himself to sit on the edge of the bed in front of her, he said, "Come here."

A tiny shuffle and she was right in front of him.

"Take off your shoes."

With one hand on his shoulder, she bent her left leg, removing one high heel, and then followed suit with the right.

"God, you're beautiful."

Her automatic response was to deny it, but the way he gazed at her actually made her feel beautiful, and if this was the one and only night they'd have together, she wasn't going to mess it up by contradicting him.

"Closer."

She stepped up, placing a leg on either side of his bent knees.

"I've been wondering about this."

"Wondering about what?"

"How you would look." His hands came around her waist, his right sliding up her ribs and around her front, softly caressing as he watched, like he was a sculptor and she was a lump of clay, his to mold into whatever form he wanted.

There was hardly any distance between them, which made it easy for Colton to lean forward and circle her nipple with his tongue. He glanced up at her. "Wondering how you would taste."

He bent to suck her nipple into his mouth.

Instinct had Ashley arching, forcing her chest to rise up against Colton's hot mouth. She threaded her fingers through his short hair, needing something to hold on to.

He flicked her left nipple back and forth with his tongue before covering the entire bud with his mouth and sucking again. It was like a string was pulled taut, some three-way cord inside of her that connected her nipple to her throat and was also strung down to the tip of her clit. Each nibble, every little bit of suction and flick of the tongue had immediate and similar effects on these connected parts of her body.

"Colton," she said his name, not really knowing why, but needing to express something.

He moved to her other nipple, leaving the left one damp and hard. Not quite as gentle now, the suction of his mouth was warm and fierce, the nibbles more like bites, his strong arms holding her as if he was never going to let her go.

Not that Ashley wanted to leave. No. Quite the opposite. She sank down onto his lap, her legs straddling his, her hot pussy snugged right up against the fly of his dress pants.

In this new position, his warm lips sought hers, kissing her with as much abandon as he'd kissed her breasts while she blindly undid the buttons on his shirt. She knew what lay beneath that starched cotton. Solid, male muscle. And while she'd touched him, she couldn't wait to *feel* him. Skin to skin. Hard muscle versus soft breasts. She couldn't wait to taste, the skin of his neck, the firm flesh of his pecs, the sweet flavor of his abdomen and navel.

Finally his shirt was undone, and she spread it wide, pushing it off his shoulders. His skin was hot and hard and felt better than she remembered as she pressed herself against him. His mouth moved with more intensity, sucking her lower lip into his before thrusting his tongue inside. Deep.

Yes.

Those bits of her that were connected by a cord responded. Her nipples tightened, and her clit throbbed with the pressure of his tongue in her mouth. She ground her pelvis down into him, needing friction. Needing more.

"Ash…"

"Yes."

Just like on the dance floor, all it took was a little pressure from his hand on her thigh and she knew what he wanted. She crawled over him onto the bed, flopping down onto her back, her legs still twined around his waist. He turned and moved between her parted legs, sliding his hands up beneath her skirt.

"As hot as this dress looks…it needs to come off."

Ash lifted her ass and reached behind to open the hidden zipper at the back of the skirt. Once done, Colton tugged, pulling the dress off her legs and tossing it to the floor.

"Look at you."

Ashley couldn't believe how satisfying it was to be lying there while Colton Cross gazed down at her with desire.

Seriously.

After making a grumbling sound deep inside his chest, he leaned over her and licked a line from her belly button up between her breasts to a sensitive spot just below her jaw.

God, it felt so good. His mouth was so hot and wet, and he seemed to know intuitively all of her erogenous zones. She grappled blindly between them for his belt buckle, her hands shaking as she fumbled with the clasp until she finally managed to get it undone. His zipper practically unzipped itself, giving her space to reach inside. She worked her hand beneath the cotton of his boxers until finally...

Oh, yes.

Gloriously aroused male flesh.

She gripped him, marveling at how soft his skin was, how hard he was beneath that satiny skin. How incredibly hot it was that his tip was wet with arousal.

For her.

She moved her hand up, then down. Repeating the process, faster and faster until Colton moaned against her neck.

Then he bit her.

"You have any idea what you're doing to me right now?" Propped on one arm, he reached down and took her hand away.

Ashley rolled her head back and forth across the pillow as she attempted to get her hand back inside his pants, but he wrestled it away. Grasping her wrist, he hoisted her hand above her head and pinned her down.

"Why don't I show you?"

9

ASHLEY PARTED HER lips to speak, but no words came out, only soft little pants as she gazed into Colton's dark eyes.

"Don't move."

It was a command. Bossy and controlling and yet Ashley loved it. Loved being told what to do. Loved feeling vulnerable to this man.

He paused a moment, as if testing her, and when she licked her lips, his gaze faltered, and he lowered himself for a kiss.

God, she could get lost in his mouth. His kisses were so all-consuming, tongue, teeth, lips, moving in a deliciously damp dance of passion until Colton pulled away, scowling down at her.

"I told you not to move."

Oops. Her hands had somehow found their way around his neck and into his hair. He gently extricated them and placed them authoritatively above her head again. Pressing her body into the mattress beneath him, he said, "I want to show you what it's like to be tortured. If you move again, I'll have to tie you down."

Ashley's eyes went wide. Not because she was shocked or offended, but because the idea of being tied down by Colton while he did wicked things to her was incredibly thrilling.

"Is that what you want?" he asked.

Were her thoughts so transparent?

"I'll be good," she said in between panting breaths.

"We'll see." He rubbed his stubbled cheek against hers before ducking lower to suck on her neck, nibbling a line down to her collarbone.

She gave herself up to his kisses, his touches, leaving her arms above her head as if she was still pinned, arching her back as he kissed his way to her breasts, paying attention to each nipple equally before moving lower and then lower still.

"These are nice." He fit a finger beneath the waistband of her panties, her good black satin ones, and ran it along her stomach.

Ash couldn't help it. She strained her hips forward, needing him to reach lower. Desperate for him to touch her, to feel her warmth and see how aroused she was. But apparently Colton liked to tease, because he removed his finger and circled the elastic that lined her right leg and then her left.

He moved lower, so that his mouth was in line with her pelvis. This time, it was his tongue that teased beneath the elastic, not his finger.

"Colton," she murmured as she raised her hips. "Please."

Colton ignored her pleas.

He grasped a knee and bent it, spreading her before ducking down to bite the taut cord at the junction of her thigh and pelvis.

She moaned.

His mouth moved to cover her mound and he breathed hot, wet air through the satin of her panties. It was exquisite.

"Please," she begged.

His teeth grazed her, and she cried out while her hips bucked up from the mattress. Colton fit his hands beneath her ass and lifted her, abrading his stubbled cheek against her thighs, tugging down on the front of her panties and rubbing himself against the front of her.

Ashley had never experienced anything like it. The friction on all her most intimate places, the sight of him lying between her parted legs, the expression of raw passion she saw on his face right after he yanked her panties off and gazed down at her exposed flesh.

"Colton?"

Did he even hear her? She couldn't tell because he was so focused on her parted thighs, spreading her legs wide enough for him to lie between, sucking on the sensitive skin high up on her leg, leaving a trail of delicious red marks.

Until finally, finally his mouth found her damp heat. His thumbs spreading her so that his tongue could lap along her swollen slit, sucking on her clit before plunging inside.

Ashley couldn't stand it. She screamed his name. Grappled with his shoulders, but the man was just too strong and too intent on what he was doing. She'd never felt so helplessly consumed by all encompassing pleasure.

She begged. She pleaded.

"Please, Colt, please."

He ignored her as he sucked and licked her into a moaning, writhing mass of boneless, orgasmic flesh. Every cell in her body lit up, tingling and jolting with intense pleasure. The three-way cord that had connected her clit to her nipples and throat grew exponentially, forming connections to her toes, the backs of her knees, the midpoint of her forehead, her entire spine and the top of her head.

Ashley didn't come; she exploded. If not for Colton's big body holding her she would have fallen apart, shattering into a million pieces, unable to put herself back together again. And it wasn't until many moments later as she gasped raggedly, trying to find herself, that she realized she was lying ensconced in Colton's arms, her head nestled on his shoulder beneath his chin as he stroked her back and murmured, "Shh," softly.

HOLY HELL. COLTON had never seen a woman come so hard. In fact, he wasn't convinced he hadn't hurt her because she whimpered and moaned like she was on the verge of tears and might actually fall apart.

That's when he'd decided to stop.

Oh, his cock was *not* happy with him. Not one bit. But it didn't matter how desperately he wanted to seat himself deep inside her gorgeous little body; he needed to know she was okay. And having her lie in his arms, her slender legs twined between his, her hand clutching at his shoulder while she got her breathing under control made him feel...

Something.

He wasn't sure what.

She made a little stuttering, breathy sound, and he instinctively drew her in closer, tucking her head beneath his chin as he caressed her back.

After a long drawn breath, she said, "I'm sorry. I—"

"No. *I'm* sorry."

Pushing herself up on to her elbow so that she could look at him, she said, "Why are you sorry?"

"I took things too far. I thought you were enjoying it and then, I don't think you did."

She blinked a few times as she studied him. "Are you kidding me?"

"No."

"Colton, I totally... I mean, I've never..." She shut her mouth and swallowed, rolling her eyes to the roof of the trailer before trying again. "What I mean is, I haven't actually...ever..." She stopped again to take a deep breath.

"No one's ever gone down on you?" he asked.

Her brows drew together. "No, I've done *that*."

"What is it, then?"

Her lips formed a firm line, as if she didn't want to say it, but then suddenly she blurted the words out anyway. "I've never orgasmed like that."

"Ever?"

She frowned, and the Ashley from the pub made an appearance, displeasure flitting across her features. "Colton. I've had an *orgasm*… It's just…" She paused, huffing.

"Sorry if I'm being dense here, but I have no idea what you are trying to say."

"I've never had one—" she gestured between them "—with a partner."

It was Colton's turn to blink in surprise. "No guy has ever brought you to orgasm?"

She shook her head.

"I'm your first?" Why did that thought give him such pleasure?

"Yeah." She scowled. "But don't let it go to your head. I imagine you've had plenty of practice."

He ignored her snide remark. "So, let me get this straight." He flexed his arms and clasped his hands behind his head in male pride. "I'm the first man to make Ashley Ozark come. Do I get a prize?"

Her expression was stormy, yet there was a softness around her mouth that told him she wasn't as upset with him and his cocky behavior as she might be leading him to believe.

"Yeah, well, there's a first and last for everything." She sat up and threw her legs over the bed. Finding her panties, she slipped them on and then snatched her dress and held it up in front of her as if she didn't want him to see her naked body even though he'd had an up close and extremely intimate view of her only moments before.

"Where do you think you're going?"

"We've both got an early morning."

He sat up and reached for her hand. "But we're not done

here. I plan on making you come at least two more times. Preferably with me inside of you."

She sucked in a breath as if the notion was shocking.

"Sounds good, doesn't it?"

"Look," she said, backing away from the bed, her dress in front of her like some kind of shield. "I know I promised some things——" her gaze flicked to his erection, lingering for a couple of heartbeats before settling back on his face "——but I can't. I need to go."

Though it pained him to bend over, he managed to do so, grabbing his boxers from the floor and pulling them on. "I'll give you a ride."

"No," she said as she backed through the door. "I'll walk. I need the fresh air."

Well, that wasn't happening, but he wasn't about to argue with her when she was so skittish. He waited for her to get dressed in the tiny bathroom, and when she came out a couple of minutes later, he was dressed himself and ready to go.

"I'm driving you home."

He could see she wanted to argue, but then she glanced at the high heels hanging from her fingertips and she nodded her assent. "Okay, only if you promise me one thing."

"Sure."

"No talking about any of this on the drive home."

"O-kay."

"Oh, and Colton?"

"Yeah?"

"We're breaking up tomorrow."

ASHLEY BARELY SLEPT, and when she did manage to fall asleep she was plagued by dreams of Colton chasing her through the forest while she fled, completely naked. Just like in bad horror movies, she inevitably tripped.

He pounced.

She woke up.

Pressing her palms to her tired, sand-papery eyes, she decided to just get up and do some work. There were pictures to download from her camera, which she'd have to pick up from Jasmine first, then she'd sort them and clean them up in Photoshop. She'd promised Ed over at *Half Moon Weekly* that she'd get pictures to him by tomorrow morning for the Wednesday paper. Plus the rodeo committee wanted images for the Half Moon webpage as soon as possible.

Half an hour later, she was standing at the door to Jasmine's room.

"Oh, hey, Ash," Jazz said, peeking around the door before opening it and covering up a yawn as she let Ash in.

"Sorry to wake you."

"No problem." Jazz located the camera bag and handed it off to Ash.

"Thank you so much," Ash said. "I really owe you."

Jazz shook her head. "No. You don't. I just hope you had fun last night."

"Oh. Um…" Ash felt her cheeks warm. "Yeah. It was good."

"That man is a god in bed, isn't he?"

"Well, I wouldn't go that far," Ash said. Some weird part of her that was loyal to Colton—probably her vagina—called her a liar. She cleared her throat. "You want to go for breakfast?"

"No. I'm going back to bed. Jazzy had a late night." She yawned again.

"Okay. I'll catch up with you at the rodeo?"

"Sure thing."

Ash was about to leave when Jazz leaned over and hugged her. "Enjoy your time with Colt while you can. You don't know how lucky you are."

Feeling like a supreme shit for all the lies she was telling, Ashley hurried home and then poured herself a bowl of cereal and settled in front of her computer, downloading all of yesterday's images on to her computer. Work. That's what she needed to do to forget all the lies.

Only thing was, all the pictures blurred into a mass of color because Colton's face monopolized her brain, a dark expression of desire and passion imprinted on his features as he kissed her. The memory alone was enough to have her rubbing her knees together, creating friction in response to the vivid memory.

I plan on making you come at least two more times. Preferably with me inside of you.

Ashley shut her eyes and rocked in her chair. If Colton could make her lose herself with just his mouth, what on earth would have happened if she'd had sex with him? What if she came while he was inside of her?

She squeezed the bridge of her nose. She'd never felt so…out of control. So vulnerable. So much at a man's mercy.

It was both wonderful and terrible.

She never wanted to experience that loss of control again. Yet, she simultaneously wanted *desperately* to lose it while Colton was inside of her.

"I'm screwed," she whispered to herself as she stared blankly at her computer screen. "Good thing this is all going to end today."

Her stomach plummeted at the thought, and Ashley gave up trying to work and instead opted for a shower.

It was many hours later, after she'd finally talked herself into getting some work done, that Ashley made her way over to the fairgrounds for the last day of the celebration. Everything was much more subdued, probably lots of people nursing hangovers, and the weather was warm for May.

She didn't even realize she was on the lookout for Colton until she saw him walking toward her from the rodeo grounds. His gait—a long, sturdy stride—was unmistakable, even though his features were unidentifiable beneath the brim of his hat. She stopped and waited, concentrating only on slowing her breathing, hoping it would have a similar effect on her racing pulse.

"Hey there, Ash."

"Colton." Ashley was impressed with how calm she sounded.

"How you doing?"

"Fine. You?"

He rubbed his jaw. "Fine."

Okay, this was a ridiculous conversation, considering the man's tongue had been doing unspeakable things to her body only twelve hours ago. She gulped.

"So, today's the day."

"Yeah. I ride at four. Last event of the day."

She shook her head, realizing he wasn't on the same page as her. Of course not. He probably had mind-blowing oral sex with all of the women he saw. This was nothing new to him.

"Good luck."

"Thanks."

"Listen." She put her hand on his chest and instantly regretted it because she also—may have—stroked his pec muscles a little in the process. "Er... I have an idea." She dropped her hand, though it still tingled from the contact.

"Oh, yeah?" He pushed his hat back, a wicked gleam now visible in his brown eyes. "Does it involve that striptease you owe me?"

Ashley's mouth fell open, and it took her a minute before she was able to manage the word "No."

"Damn."

"I'm going to send Brandi your way after your ride. Flirt with her. Then I'll have a reason for breaking up with you."

A muscle twitched along his jaw as he studied her. "You sure you want to do that?"

"Yep. Positive."

He took a step toward her. She backed up, nearly tripping. A flash from her stupid dream where she fell and he pounced, taking her breath away.

Grabbing her hand to steady her, he didn't let go. No. In fact, he pulled her forward right up against his chest. "How about a farewell kiss, then?"

Ashley pressed her lips together so she wouldn't be tempted. "I don't think that's a good idea."

"You know what I think?"

She shook her head. Slowly.

He leaned close and whispered, "I think you think too much." Then he kissed her, using his tongue, and reminding her very graphically of what happened between them last night.

Ashley moaned into his mouth.

"Hey, you two," a chipper voice called from behind her.

Ash tried to pull away, but Colton didn't let up right away. He finished the kiss, giving her a final soft, lingering one before releasing her.

A last kiss.

"Hey, Jasmine," he said over her shoulder.

Ashley's legs felt like noodles, and she was grateful for Colton's arm around her waist for purely gravitational reasons.

"How was the rest of the party?" Ash asked.

"Good. It was fun. Really great." Jasmine smiled. This time Ashley was sure it was forced.

"Listen, ladies," Colton said, sliding his arm out from Ashley's waist. "I promised to help out with the stock. Catch up with you later?"

"Yes. For sure," Jasmine said.

Colton tipped his hat and turned to walk away.

"Bye, Colton," Ashley called.

He didn't turn around but simply held his hand up in a backward wave. And that, Ashley realized, would be the last time they were together as pretend boyfriend and girlfriend.

10

ASHLEY STARED AFTER Colton's retreating back as an overwhelming sense of disappointment engulfed her.

"You are so lucky," Jasmine said, a wistful tone in her voice.

This charade could not go on, and while she had some weird mixed-up feelings about it ending, she also looked forward to not having to pretend in front of Jasmine anymore. Speaking of which, there was something wrong with her friend. "Okay, Jazz. Spill."

"It's nothing."

"Jazz…"

After a big breath, she said, "Parker's going to London for business. That's all."

"Are you joining him?"

"No. He said he's going to be too busy."

"How long is he gone?"

"A week." Suddenly Jasmine's cuticles were of great interest as she studied her hands.

"Why don't you go and surprise him?"

Without glancing up, her friend said, "Showing up in London unannounced would *not* go over well." She sighed. "Parker is *not* Colton."

Out of nowhere a hot poker stabbed the inside of Ashley's gut. Oh, if only Jasmine knew the truth of it.

"So, I was thinking…" Jasmine hazarded a wobbly

smile as she finally met Ashley's gaze. "Maybe I'll just stay on for a few extra days...or a week. What do you think?"

Weird shit started happening in Ashley's chest so that when she said, "Really?" the second syllable sounded super high.

"Yeah." Jazz shrugged, shaking herself out of the funk she'd just been in. "I mean, why not, right? Then you and I can have a proper visit without you having to work all the time. I can get to know Colton better." She glanced toward the rodeo grounds, though Colton had already disappeared. "And, you can help me with the wedding plans." She took Ashley's hands and squeezed, her smile losing its melancholy tinge.

That was the thing about Jasmine. Even when she was down, she had this freakish ability to turn it around into something positive, making everything okay. It's why Ashley both loved her and—well—sometimes found her hard to take.

No one could possibly be that positive all the time, could they?

"Say yes," Jasmine urged.

"Of course," Ashley replied. Really, what other reply was there? *Sorry, I can't because I have a fake boyfriend, and we're supposed to break up later today?*

"Oh, good!" Jasmine pulled her in for a hug. "It'll be so fun. Just like old times. Who wants to go to London when I can spend time with my best friend instead?"

Ashley hugged back, realizing it was a genuine hug of relief. Partly because she was looking forward to spending time with Jasmine but mostly because it meant she *wouldn't* have to break up with Colton today after all.

Focus.

Colton breathed in slowly and out slowly.

There was nothing but the flexing and snorting of the bull beneath him, the rasp of the rope around his gloved hand, the clanking of the metal gates as the animal struggled in the confined space and the voice of the gate operator.

"You ready, Colt?"

He was about to nod when he glanced up. Across from the chute was the announcer's stand, and standing on one side was the slight figure of a woman, camera poised in front of her face.

"Colt?"

"Hmm?"

"You set?"

He shifted on the bull's back, finding his seat, or trying to at the very least. He drew in another slow, deep breath, tugged on the rope, testing his grip, and said, "Yep. I'm good."

The gate opened, the animal reacted, and Colt held on as the animal leaped into the air, legs kicking, body twisting and contorting beneath him. When the bull twisted right, Colt flowed to the left, when its hind quarter bucked, he leaned back. Colton's trick had always been to imagine himself as part of the animal, an extension that moved fluidly, balancing with the beast, not moving against it.

Sort of like dancing with Ashley or kissing her while her body bucked beneath him...

His spine jarred, his hand slipped and Colton lost his seat just moments before the horn sounded. He fell with a thud on to his back in the dirt, dazed and staring up at the blue sky. He tried to suck in a breath, but nothing came.

What the fuck just happened?

The sound of horse hooves jolted him into awareness, and Colton scrambled to his feet, sprinting for the gate in instinct to avoid getting trampled or gored. Once safely on the other side of the fence, he glanced toward the announcer's stage. Ashley stared back, her eyes wide, her face pale, and at that moment a whole slew of random emotions infiltrated his psyche: bitterness that she'd distracted him. Worry that he'd scared her. Longing to take her in his arms to comfort her and disappointment that he wouldn't get another chance to do that.

He broke her gaze and turned to walk slowly to the competitors' tent on the other side of the stands. Every muscle in his body ached, including something deep inside of his chest.

"Sorry about the ride." His brother, Dillon, squeezed him gently on the shoulder. "I thought you had Braggin' Rights licked."

"I did." Colt shrugged. "Or, I should have. He's not the toughest one out there."

"What happened?"

"Distracted." Colton grabbed two chilled bottles of water out of a tub of ice and passed one to his brother.

"It happens."

Not to him, he was going to say. Except that, obviously, it had happened to him, dammit.

There was a food tent set up where volunteers were serving beef on a bun to the competitors. Colton stood in the short line to grab some grub. "You want anything?" he asked Dillon.

"Naw. I'm good. We've got a big meal planned back at the ranch. Speaking of, you heading back tonight or tomorrow morning?"

"Tonight."

Dillon nodded. "Okay. See you later, then."

Colton sat at one of the picnic tables, devouring half of the bun in one bite. This weekend hadn't gone quite as planned. Not that he typically had a plan for rodeo weekends, but winning the bull-riding event was a given. Being distracted by some woman who was all slim limbs and hot kisses, was not.

Good thing he was done with all that. No point staying at the trailer tonight. He'd have to get up extra early to be out at the ranch for chores tomorrow. And, seeing as he didn't win the contest, he wasn't keen to stick around for the awards that would be happening later this evening. That was just throwing salt on the wound.

"Hi, Colton."

He glanced up. Ashley's sister Brandi took a seat on the bench opposite him.

He sighed. Showtime.

"Hello." He shoved the remainder of the bun into his mouth, wiped his lips and fingers with the paper napkin after swallowing and said, "What can I do for you, Brandi?"

He was not in the mood for this. Not in the mood to flirt with a woman he wasn't interested in, but neither was he in the mood to be some other woman's pawn in a warped game of jealousy and pretend. He was tired of being used and, frankly, done with the whole sham.

"I wanted to talk about Ashley."

Of course she did. And, like clockwork, Ashley and Jasmine rounded the back of the bleachers heading their way. He finished the water in the bottle and squeezed the plastic, finding pleasure in the crinkly sound it made as he crushed it.

Pretending like he didn't see Ashley coming, he said, "You sure you want to talk about Ashley when you're here, looking so good?" Only thing was, he sounded condescending when he said it, and Brandi's look of confusion told him he wasn't believable.

So, he slid his hand across the picnic table and touched hers, making a crisscross pattern over the top.

"What are you doing?" She snatched her hand away.

Ashley stood beside him now; he could smell her orange-blossom scent. She cleared her throat.

"Oh, hi, Ashley," he said. Seeing her brought on that same rush of conflicting emotions he'd experienced right after his ride. Which was why when Ashley shook her head in short, sharp little movements, he couldn't figure out what she wanted.

Her gaze flicked meaningfully from her sister and back to him.

Colton frowned. What the hell did that mean? Did she want him to flirt right in front of her?

"So, Brandi...uh, what are you doing—?"

"Um, Colt, can I talk to you?" Ashley interrupted.

Maybe he was still dazed from being thrown from a bull, but Colton was confused. Did Ashley want him to hit on her sister now or not?

Grabbing his sleeve, she tugged him into a standing position. "What the hell are you doing?" she seethed once she dragged him far enough away so as not to be overheard.

"Doing what you asked me to do."

"Argh." She stomped around the side of the event tent and waited for him on the other side where they were out of sight of the picnic table.

"What?" Colton asked.

Ashley leaned against the corner pole, her arms crossed in front of her chest. Did she have any idea that the placement of her arms caused a little gap between the material of her shirt?

Jesus.

He should not be looking down Ashley's shirt.

"She's staying," she said as way of an explanation.

"What? Who's staying?" Colton tilted his head, trying to get a better view.

"Jasmine. She's not leaving tomorrow."

"So?"

"So, I—" Ashley took a deep breath and then pushed it out. "Are you looking down my shirt?"

Colton's head snapped up. "No."

Her lips twisted, as if his indiscretion was flattering, not annoying. After adjusting her stance, Ashley continued, "I need you to pretend a little while longer."

"Is that so?" Colton braced a hand on the pole above her head.

"Yes."

"For how long?"

"I don't know. A couple more days..." Her words trailed off.

"That's it?"

"A week, maybe?"

"A week?" Colton coughed—or maybe laughed—into his fist.

"Don't laugh."

"You realize you will owe me big-time if you want me for a week."

She flinched. Couldn't really blame her. He hadn't meant it to sound so cocky. But for whatever reason, the thought of pretending for a while longer gave him great pleasure. In fact, it even took away some of the sting from his failed ride.

"How, exactly, will I owe you?" she asked, the words coming out individually on each breath of air.

Did she realize her hands were on his chest? Was she aware her fingers were fiddling with the buttons on his shirt?

Which was just the way it should be, back to Ashley needing him and Colton finding creative ways to make her pay.

"Let's just say I'm going to up the ante," Colton said, watching her fingers on his shirt.

"Oh, yeah?"

"Yes."

"Like…?"

"Expect to pay me back in appropriately *inappropriate* ways."

Ashley gasped, a pleasing, sexy sound.

Colton lifted her chin and licked across her lips. "Bring Jasmine out to the ranch tomorrow, and we can discuss this in more detail."

Before Ash could go back to her friend, Colton added in a hoarse whisper, "And you can bet it'll involve making you come so hard you won't know up from down."

"OH, MY GOD! It's perfect!"

Ashley, Jasmine and Gloria were all congregated on the deck of the Silver Tree Guest ranch on Monday afternoon, gazing out at the spectacular view of the pond and forest with a backdrop of majestic peaks. Even the heavy gray storm clouds building to the west added to the dramatic landscape.

Jasmine held her arms wide as she took in the surroundings. "I *have* to have the wedding here. I just have to."

Gloria waddled to her side, phone in hand. "Let me check the calendar. Okay?" She tapped into it. "We've got a few open weekends this summer, if that's not too soon." She showed the phone to Jasmine, and the two of them discussed dates.

Meanwhile, Ashley pretended not to be staring at the open barn door where she'd seen Colton disappear a few minutes ago. If this was all for pretend, why was it that the mere thought of him or the recollection of his last statement to her, *you can bet it'll involve making you come so hard you won't know up from down*, had her heart racing, her palms sweating and her clit throbbing.

Yes, her clit.

"Yes!" Jasmine gushed, as if privy to Ashley's thoughts.

"I think that'll work." She tugged on Ashley's arm. "What do you think of August 7?"

She coughed. "Yeah. Sounds good."

"You won't be gone by then?"

Oh. Right. Weird how she hadn't thought about her big plan of moving away. Of starting her new venture—a photo blog—since…when? All this stuff with Colton?

"Um…" Ash cleared her throat. "No, I'll be here for the summer. Working."

"Wonderful." Gloria confirmed the date in her calendar, and when she was done, she said, "I know you've been staying at the Gold Dust in town, but if you're interested, you can stay out here for the next few days and get a feel for the place. We can plan everything in that time. What do you think?"

"Oh, my God! That's exactly what we'll do." She gave Ashley a happy, hopeful look. "And you'll stay out here, too, right?"

Ash gulped. Stay out at the ranch? Dear God. Why did that thought please her so much? "Sure. I'd love to."

"Great, I'll go make up a couple of guest rooms while you two make yourselves at home."

"We'll only need one," Jazz corrected as Gloria waddled toward the door to the house. "Ash will be staying with Colton, I'm sure."

"Who will be staying with me?"

Really? The man himself *had* to be right there, on the other side of the deck, looking manly in his work clothes, his collar open, his sleeves rolled up, showing off all the deliciously ripped muscles and tendons in his forearms.

"Ashley, of course," Jasmine said.

"You don't have to work this week?" Colton asked, nudging his hat back. If not for the wicked gleam in his eyes, she would have been wondering if he was trying to get out of having an unwanted houseguest.

"Oh. Um. Just a couple of shifts at the flower shop. But, ah…"

"That's right," Jazz enthused. "I forgot you work at the flower shop, too." She clapped her hands. "So, that's where I'll get the flowers. My God, Ash. Do you realize how easy you're making this for me?"

Ashley gulped as her gaze met Colton's. How ironic that Jasmine thought she was making it easy for her when Jasmine was the one making things a little too easy for her and Colton to finish what they'd started the other night.

"I'm going to go take some pictures to send to Parker," Jazz said. "Then let's head back to town to pick up our stuff." She scurried off into the lodge, phone in hand.

"So now you're staying out here?" Colton asked as he climbed the steps to the deck. "In my bunkhouse?"

"Looks like it."

"Were you going to ask me if it was okay or just show up in my bed?"

She tilted her head to look up at him. "It was literally just decided the minute you walked up. I don't have to stay with you if—"

He shut her up with a kiss, soft and sweet. "No. I want you in my bed, Ashley. We've got some unfinished business, you and I."

His hot breath tickled her ear, and somehow her fingers had become tangled in between the buttons on his shirt, her fingertips grazing the warm skin of his chest, sending shivers from her hands up her arms and settling somewhere between her shoulder blades.

"You're not going to run away this time, are you?"

"No. I owe you," she said softly, thinking of the various ways she could pay him back. Another massage? A home-cooked meal? Something a little more…personal?

"You got that right." Colton gazed down at her. "But I don't want you there just because you owe me."

She bunched his shirt up in her fists. "Why do you want me there?"

He lowered his lids and in a gruff voice said, "Because I need to see you come again."

AFTER SPENDING THE weekend away, there were tons of chores to catch up on, particularly with all the new calves this spring. Colton and Curtis were out in the pasturelands when the rain that had threatened all day came, slanting down in sheets, which made everything take longer. By the time he got back to his side of the bunkhouse, it was too late to join the family in the main house for dinner, so he showered and grabbed a quick meal in his own kitchenette.

He'd no sooner done the washing up before there was a bold knock on his door. Swiping the grin from his face with the damp tea towel, he hung it on the hook by the sink and took his time making his way to the door. Nothing like building anticipation. Making the woman wait.

He opened the door, and there she was, wearing a trench coat and soaked through, gazing up at him through damp hair and beneath long lashes. Not shy—like she'd been at his trailer. Not disdainful—like she'd been at the bar.

Coy.

Her smile was that secret, sexy one he liked.

"Well, hiya, Ashley. What can I do for you?"

She placed a hand on his chest and pushed him aside so she could enter. "It's not what you can do for me," she said huskily over her shoulder. "Rather, what I can do for you."

Whoa.

Who was this woman?

Colton couldn't wait to find out. He closed the door behind her—and locked it—before leaning against it. Crossing one boot over the other, he also crossed his arms over his chest, waiting.

She stood in the middle of his sitting room, looking

around before slowly turning. "I'm wet," she said matter-of-factly.

"You are."

"Do you mind if I take off my coat?"

"Please." Colton waved a hand in her direction.

One side of her mouth tipped up as she slowly undid the ties at her waist. Then, without breaking eye contact, she undid her jacket, button by button, until there were no buttons left. She held the sides of her jacket together, only loosening the top, revealing—quite splendidly—that all she was wearing underneath was lingerie.

Black, lacy lingerie.

She turned to the side, gazed coyly over her shoulder and loosened the jacket, letting it dip low, so that her back and the top of her ass were bared. The only thing covering her pale skin was the thin straps of her bra and the T at the back of her thong panties. She dropped the coat and stood there, back arched like a swimsuit model, biting her lip while she peered over her shoulder in her delicious undies and high-heeled black boots.

Holy mother of fuck.

"Do you want me to finish this here? Or in your bedroom?"

Colton's mouth went dry. He didn't bother to answer and instead moved toward her, hands itching to touch.

But when he was still a few steps away, she held out a hand to stop him.

"Nope. No touching. Not till I say so."

Oh, baby.

Who the hell was this woman and what had she done with uptight Ashley Ozark?

Colton didn't know. Didn't care.

He brushed past her on his way to the bedroom. "Let's finish this in here."

"As you wish."

11

ASHLEY WAS IMPRESSED with herself for how calm she sounded, considering her insides felt like a soda can that had been shaken up, fizzy and in need of release in a big, big way.

Pop my top, Colton Cross.

She shivered.

What the hell was she doing? It had all started on the drive back to town to gather her things when Ash had been pretending to listen to Jasmine jabbering on about wedding plans. Meanwhile, she'd secretly been thinking about Colton. Her relationship—or rather non-relationship, as it were—with the cowboy.

After dropping Jasmine off and agreeing to meet back at the ranch later that night in their own vehicles, she'd realized two things. The first thing was, she did not feel like she had one iota of control in this non-relationship. That had to change. Pronto. The second thing was—and this was the weird part because it directly contradicted the first part—she wanted to absolutely, completely and utterly *lose control* to Colton Cross.

How was that even possible?

She didn't know.

All she knew was that she wanted Colton to touch her in ways she'd never let another man touch her. She wanted to respond to him like she'd never responded to another.

She wanted Colton to do wicked and wonderful things to her until she lost it.

Like in the trailer.

The problem was she wanted all those things without losing herself to him. Which didn't make sense. But then, nothing about what she and Colton were doing made sense.

So when the clouds that had threatened to let loose all day finally opened up into a soaking spring storm, she reminded herself to grab her rainproof trench coat...and an idea hit.

The striptease.

She'd obsessed about it the whole day of the party; in fact, she'd thought about it so much, she'd had the whole thing planned out, had even practiced in front of her bedroom mirror. How to move, how to smile, how to gaze wantonly from below half-closed lids. Yes, she had looked utterly ridiculous, batting her lashes at herself in the mirror. Until she'd closed her eyes and pretended her hands were Colton's and it was him caressing her body, not her.

Ashley was certain that following through with the striptease would accomplish that weird paradox she was going for. Giving her control while simultaneously giving Colton leave to make her come apart again.

Of course, now that she was standing in Colton's bunkhouse in her very best pair of underwear and a stolen pair of Brandi's thigh-high boots, she was beginning to have her doubts.

"You coming?" his voice rumbled from the dark bedroom.

"You need an exercise in patience, mister," she called with way more self-assurance than she felt.

Wasn't that the key? Fake it until you make it, right?

His grumbling response made her smile.

See?

She was in control.

She moved across the room, wobbling only once in the high heels—thank God Colton didn't see—and then propped herself up in the doorway, a hand on either side of the frame, striking a pose she'd practiced in the mirror, hoping it looked sexy and not stupid. By the expression on Colton's face, she'd miraculously managed the first.

"Do you need music?" he asked. He was lying on his bed, his boots crossed at the ankles, his hands behind his head, all casual-like.

But the bulge at his crotch did not lie.

Shaking her head, she said, "No. Not unless you want it."

"Nope."

She glided into the room. Hard to do in the boots, but it was a small room, and she thought she'd pulled it off pretty well, coming to stand at the foot of his bed. Gazing directly into Colton's eyes, Ashley ran a hand over her stomach, making back and forth passes just below her breasts. She'd practiced this maneuver, too, though at home, she'd imagined her hands were Colton's, which was hard to do when she was watching said cowboy.

So she closed her eyes, trying to recapture the feeling she'd experienced at home, gliding her hand up over her breasts to her throat, her thumb running along her jawline before skirting her mouth. Parting her lips on the next pass, she licked her thumb, pretending it was Colton's. The fact that Colton uttered harsh sounds of desire from so close by helped make her fantasy much more real.

"You are one sexy woman," Colton rumbled.

God.

What had seemed so ridiculous in her bedroom now seemed incredibly...hot. She opened her eyes, daring to check Colton's expression.

Intense and brooding.

He had one knee propped up, and, while his left hand was still behind his head, his right rested on his belt buckle.

Holding his gaze, Ash slid the tips of her fingers beneath the cup of her bra. Sweet mercy, her nipple was sensitive. She pinched and flinched from the crazy sensations that skittered across her chest and abdomen.

"How about I tell you what to do," Colton suggested. He popped the oval buckle on his belt and moved it to the side.

"How about you lie there, watch the show and stay quiet?" Ashley responded. Was that really her voice? So low? So husky?

"Bossy."

She squeezed her own breast, sucking in a breath because it felt so good, and she ran her other hand down her stomach, slipping down to stroke the front of her panties. "It's not called a striptease for nothing."

"Mmm." Colton's hand mimicked hers, stroking himself over the denim. "Whatever you say, boss-lady."

"That's right," she said as she propped a boot up on the end of the bed, placing her hands on her calf and sliding them up the shiny surface, up past the tops to her thigh, using her short nails to gently abrade the exposed skin of her upper thigh before settling a hand between her legs.

"Just so you know, there will be payback for this." His voice was gruff as he popped the buttons on his fly.

"Payback? How can there be payback for payment?"

"You'll see."

"Shh." She rested a finger against her lips while the fingers of her other hand played with herself over the lacy material. "I said no talking."

"Just want to be clear before you go too far." The last button popped and he spread his fly wide open. "In case you're thinking about bolting again."

"I'm not going to bolt." Just as he moved his hand down the front of his boxers to stroke himself, she slid hers down inside her panties. Her skin was completely smooth. Completely bare. She'd shaved it all, just for him, another thing she'd never done for a man. Though, as she stroked herself, she had to admit that she liked it, too.

Her pussy was soft and wet, and she couldn't wait for him to see her.

But not yet.

She dipped her fingers just inside, far enough to know how aroused she was, but not so far that she'd get carried away.

"Come here." His voice was low and demanding. Her body responded to him immediately, leaning toward him as if she was a magnet and he was the North Pole. But Ashley wasn't ready to give up control yet. Not by a long shot.

"I said no talking." She wagged her finger at him, though he appeared hazy as she regarded him while still playing with her smooth self.

"And I said come here."

"Why?"

"Because I'm going to lick your fingers."

Her hand stilled as her body twitched involuntarily. Ashley did not respond, and neither did she allow herself to move around the bed to stand beside him, no matter how loud every single cell in her entire body screamed at her to do so, dying to experience the very thing he'd just said in that deep, commanding voice.

No.

She slowly drew her hand out from beneath the lace, languidly drawing those damp fingers up her body. Up, up, up until they circled her throat and jaw.

"Don't you dare," Colton growled.

Oh, yes. Yes she would dare.

First she licked her thumb.

Colton made a rumbling sound in response.

Then she circled her parted lips with her fingers.

Colton moaned.

Finally, she opened her mouth and sucked two fingers in, pulling them out only to draw them in again.

"You will pay for that."

"Mmm."

He grunted, and Ash reveled in the wonderful, delicious sensation of this unexpected power she exuded. She was driving Colton Cross to distraction by simply touching herself and denying him the opportunity to touch. It was intoxicating.

She withdrew her fingers and played with the bra strap on her shoulder. "The whole point of a striptease…" Ash whispered, flicking the left strap down, followed by the right, "is to tease."

Colton replied with a string of pretty much every obscenity there was, and Ashley covered her smile of satisfaction by lowering her leg from the bed and turning her back on him. Reaching around behind her, she unclasped her bra and let it drop.

She glanced over her shoulder to see Colton's reaction and found him sitting up, tugging off his boots, followed by the double thud of them landing on the floor, discarded.

Turning away again, Ashley arched her back while playing with the band of her panties, pushing the band down, then pulling it up again. Easing it low…slowly.

Then up.

Then back down as she gyrated her ass.

She heard the friction of denim against skin. Colton must have removed his jeans. Her pulse raced at the thought.

This time, instead of pulling the waistband of her panties back up, she inched it lower, and lower, swiveling her hips as the lace passed over the globe of her ass until the panties simply slithered to the floor.

She glanced over her shoulder.

Colton was sitting up, his shirt undone, his gaze clouded with lust.

God, this was fun.

Ash bent low to unzip her boots, unabashedly giving him a view of her bare ass, when his rumbling command stopped her.

"Don't."

Her hands stilled at the top of the zipper on the left boot. She straightened before casting a leisurely glance back at him.

His gaze was no longer cloudy but stormy.

"You've stripped." He pushed himself off the bed to stand.

"You've teased." He strode toward her, grasped her shoulders and turned her to face him.

His gaze seared her skin, lighting up every inch of her body from her lips to her nipples, from abdomen to where her hands covered her sex. He seized her wrists and pulled her hands away, forcing her to reveal herself for the first time.

"Sweet mother of God."

When his gaze met hers the storm had morphed into a full-blown hurricane, savage and wild, hell-bent on destruction.

"Now it's your turn to do as I say."

Ash swallowed with difficulty.

"And the first thing you're going to do is leave those fucking boots on."

COLTON COULDN'T REMEMBER ever being so turned on. Seriously. If someone would have told him a week ago that Ashley Ozark was a sex goddess, he'd have laughed in their face. Colton was not laughing now. Oh, no. He was on the very cusp of losing his mind. Of doing things to this woman that were still illegal in certain states.

Primal, savage things.

He needed this woman.

Now.

"Go stand by that wall," he said. "Legs wide. Hands above your head."

Ashley regarded him for the span of a heartbeat before complying—blessed girl—making the three steps that took her to the wall, placing her hands up high, and spreading her legs like she was a perp, caught in the act of some crime, about to be frisked. God, her legs looked gorgeous in those boots. Her ass was perfect, round and high. Her waist narrow. Her skin...

Lickable.

"Don't move," he commanded before opening the nightstand and removing a condom. It took him about as much time to get it out of its packaging and on to his erection as the amount of time he'd spent on the bull yesterday. Nearly eight seconds but not quite.

Two steps and he was standing right behind her, his hands taking over, needing to touch every inch of her perfect skin. He leaned into her back as his hands moved around her front.

"You've been very bad, Ms. Ozark," he whispered hotly into her ear.

"How do you figure that?"

"I don't like being teased."

"Neither do I."

His hands covered both breasts, pinching at her little nipples until they became rock-hard buds between his fingers.

"The fact you're breathing so hard indicates the opposite."

"The fact you're hard as a rock—" she wagged her ass against his cock "—would suggest the same," she countered.

Cheeky female.

She'd pay for that. He released her breasts and slid his hands down her tummy—such a nice tummy—and kneaded the taut cords at her hips, moving closer and closer to her core.

Her pretty, bare mound was more than he could take. How could her skin be so soft here? It was sweet and sexy and touchable and, good God, he wanted this woman.

He cupped her hard. Rubbing and kneading her soft flesh, getting off on the sweet pants she made in between moans of pleasure.

"Colton…" she whispered. "Oh, Colton."

"Yeah, baby?" He dug deeper, penetrating her with three fingers at once.

She cried out and tilted her pelvis back into his hand, forcing his fingers deeper than he'd meant to go.

Fitting his body flush against hers, he covered one hand where it was pressed against the wall and then guided his cock to her soaked pussy. He didn't penetrate but rather wedged his erection in between her pussy lips, rocking back and forth, creating friction along her damp slit.

"Colton! Please!"

Yes. He wanted the same thing. Only thing was, he needed to see her come this time. Because this time he was going to make her come while he was deep inside of her.

When he backed up—only for a second—she gasped in indignation.

When he flipped her around so she faced him, she gasped with surprise and something else. He was pretty damn sure it was ecstasy.

Taking hold of both her hands, he lifted them to the wall above her head and leaned down to capture her mouth, plunging his tongue past her lips like his cock longed to plunge into her smoking hot core. Biting and sucking, he ravished her mouth while his hips thrust against her, his cock sliding between her labia in deliciously frustrating friction.

Ashley's fingers curled with his, her strong hands holding tight, jerking and squeezing, as she gave her mouth just as passionately to him.

He released a hand and slid it down her arm and side to her hip. Moving lower, he grasped her knee and drew it up, opening her to him.

Pulling away, he grabbed her chin and held her still, forcing her to look at him. "You're going to wrap your legs around my waist. Do you understand?"

She blinked and then nodded.

With a hand under her ass, he lifted her, and she wrapped those glorious legs around his midsection.

"Now, I'm going to make you come." He thrust all the way inside of her.

She sucked in a breath.

"And you have to promise me something." Holding on to her bottom, he withdrew.

"What?"

"When you come—" he slammed back inside and her eyes rolled skyward "—you have to keep your eyes open." He withdrew again.

She made a mewling sound, soft and sexy.

"Ash?"

"Yeah?" The word hitched in the middle.

"Look at me."

Her nails dug into his shoulders as she blinked at him, passion making her gaze hazy. "I need to see your face when you do it." Colton grunted as he plunged inside of her again. "I need you to see me." He drove into her again and again, his words sounding more guttural with every thrust as his body gave in to its basic urges. "I need you to know who is doing this to you."

"Colton." His name was a plea, a plea to stop? A plea to

keep going? She didn't know what she wanted, he could see that from the confused pleasure on her face. Could feel it by the scratches on his back.

He needed to taste her mouth one more time because he could sense how close she was. How close he was. And he needed to be joined with her in every way. Taste her. Touch her. Experience her body from her mouth to her tight nipples to her wet channel and her clenching thighs.

She tore her mouth away to cry his name. "Colton…"

Yes. Oh, God. Yes. Say it again.

Pressing his body into hers to hold her against the wall, he drilled her harder and harder, faster and faster.

"Oh, God, Colton!"

With her ass in his hands, he held tight, turned and stumbled the three steps to the bed, lowering them both onto the mattress where he could finish properly. The second she was horizontal, her body arched into his, a bow of taut pleasure.

"Open your eyes, Ash."

She did as she was told, though he doubted whether she could actually see. Wild arousal monopolized her features, her mouth parted as she gasped for breath, air hitching in and out of her lungs.

Colt ground his teeth as he held on to her hips, moving faster, barely able to contain the mounting need to release.

"Come, baby. Come," he urged. "Let yourself go. C'mon."

She grappled at his shoulders, pushing and pulling as if she didn't know if she was coming or going until finally her body bucked, a wicked all-encompassing reflex as she keened in a way he'd only heard from wild animals in the bush.

"Look at me, dammit. Look at me," he commanded through clenched teeth.

Somehow she managed to pull her head up and stare openly into his face just as her orgasm hit. He thrust once more before holding her flush, giving himself permission to release, opening his body's floodgates so that his orgasm raced to compete with hers.

Crazy emotions flitted over her features. Pain. Joy. Pleasure. Confusion. Ecstasy.

He thrust himself deeper as his own body spasmed inside of her, and just when he thought it was over, it wasn't. One more jolt, one more spurt, one more pleasurable throb made more sweet by the pulsing of her inner walls.

"Colton..." Her voice was ragged, and again it sounded like she might cry.

Well, shit.

He lowered his body on top of her and rolled them to their sides, cradling her head against his chest, stroking her soft hair.

Damn.

It took him a while to catch his breath and to bring his heartbeat back into normal range. That's when Colton started to wonder if he'd gone too far. Pushed Ashley too much. Maybe her sex kitten act was just that, all an act.

He drew her closer, kissing the top of her head.

Ashley moved out of his embrace and propped herself up on to her elbow beside him. She gazed down at him, looking both pleased and puzzled.

"How long does it take?" she asked, her face flushed, her fine hair wild and sexy.

"How long does what take?"

She reached down between them where he was still deliciously embedded inside her body. Drawing a circle on his thigh, she asked, "For you to be ready to go again?" She met his gaze, and a small smile touched the corners of her lips. "Because I think I want to do that again."

12

ASHLEY ROLLED OUT of bed—stiffly—and went in search of her clothes. Colton had left a couple of hours ago to do chores, and she had fallen right back asleep.

I just had sex with Colton Cross, an incredulous inner voice whispered.

"That wasn't just sex," she murmured aloud. "That was… God, I don't know what that was."

Now, all she had to do was find her clothes and pretend like everything was normal. Though there was nothing about her body that felt normal. They'd had sex once more before falling asleep, and then Colton had woken her up sometime in the middle of the night…or had she woken him up? It was all a little foggy.

She found her panties hidden halfway under the bed. Her bra was a few feet away. That was it. Aside from the boots and trench coat. Pulling the curtains back from the small window in Colton's room, she peered outside. The sun shone, and steam rose up from the ground where it was wet from last night's rain.

Oh, great.

She'd been so focused on the striptease, she'd forgotten her bag in the car. Tucking the boots under her arm, she found her coat still lying on the floor in the sitting room, pulled it on and headed outside toward the parking area, carefully walking barefoot across the yard. It was early yet, so she didn't see anyone around, thankfully. Once the trunk was popped, she threw the boots into the back and grabbed her suitcase and camera bag. The second she turned around, she dropped the suitcase...

And squealed.

Colton was right there. How he'd snuck up on her, quiet as a shadow, she had no idea. His mouth quirked up in a half smile as he closed the distance between them.

"Morning, Ms. Ozark."

"Colton."

Why did it feel so weird to talk to the man who'd done more intimate things to her than any man had done before? Was it the light of day? Was it the realization of who this man really was? Cocky Colton Cross?

He reached for the collar of her coat and tugged. "What you got under there?" he asked cheerfully.

"None of your business." She slapped his hand away.

"It sure as hell was my business last night." He tugged some more and then leaned down to get a view. "This morning, too, if memory serves." He stuck a finger inside the coat, drawing a line up between her breasts.

"Colt!"

"Aw, don't tell me we're done playing." His fingers trailed up her chest and traced her collarbones, leaving dark smudges in their wake. "I'm done chores. We've got an hour before breakfast." He glanced at his hands. "I'm dirty and need a shower." Pulling open the top of her coat, he pointed at the dirty smudges he'd left. "Looks like I've gotten you all dirty, too."

Ashley couldn't help smiling. "What do you suggest?"

"Well, if I was any kind of proper host, I'd offer to wash up the mess I'd made."

"Is that so?"

"Mmm-hmm. But first, grab your bags."

Just after straightening from picking up her suitcase,

Colton stooped and scooped her—bags and all—into his arms.

"What the hell are you doing?"

"I'm carrying you back. Can't have you cutting up those sweet little feet on these sharp rocks."

"Colton." She laughed, pounding him playfully on the chest. "I won't cut my feet."

"Not now you won't," he said, striding toward the bunk-house as if she weighed nothing at all. "Besides, I like having you in my arms."

Ashley giggled and nestled her head beneath Colton's chin. Parts of her body throbbed willingly in reaction to his not-so-subtle innuendo. Parts of her brain reminded her that this wasn't real, but the reminder seemed to come from a long way away.

Anyway, so what if it wasn't real? It was fun, and besides, no one had ever worried about her sweet little feet before. Not even the romantic Spaniard from her holiday. And she'd certainly never been carried by a man before—never allowed herself to be carried. Not that she'd had any offers.

So, if this was the last and only time a man carried her to protect her feet, she was going to enjoy it.

"So, I WAS thinking maybe we could tour around the ranch after breakfast to check out locations for photo shoots," Jasmine said. "What do you think?"

"Great idea," Ash replied, realizing she'd only been stirring the food around on her plate and not eating because her mind was on a loop, replaying the events of yesterday and this morning.

Sweet Hannah.

Being carried across a gravel parking lot might be gallant, but the things Colton did to her in the shower were anything but.

Soaping her body.

Using the removable shower head to rinse her body.

Using the vibrating spray to arouse her body.

Using his fingers and mouth to tease her body.

Making her wait until after the shower to fill her body.

Yes. Colton filled her like she'd never experienced before. So...thoroughly. So satisfying...

The toe of a boot touched the inside of her calf, and she jerked.

The man who was currently starring in an erotic scene in her mind was sitting beside her, playing footsies with her.

Or bootsies.

"If you like," Colton said, "I can saddle up some horses. Take you around to all the best spots."

"That sounds fun," Ash said eagerly, her hand landing on Colton's thigh beneath the table.

"Oh." Jasmine frowned. "Thanks for the offer, but I'm not much for horses."

Ash had forgotten that Jasmine didn't ride. Not that she rode a ton herself, but she had always enjoyed it when she got the chance. Plus, the idea of spending the day with Colton, doing stuff that didn't involve getting naked, was surprisingly appealing.

Though the naked stuff was appealing, too.

"What about the quads?" Colton asked. "You opposed to four-by-fouring?"

"Can a quad fit three people?" Jasmine asked.

"Nah. But I'll ask Curtis if he wants to come along for a couple hours." Colton nodded at Dillon. "You can spare us this morning, can't you?"

"Sure," Dillon said. "Just make sure you're back this afternoon. We've got some fence to fix."

Jasmine had a contemplative look on her features as

she blinked at Colton. "You sure Curtis won't mind?" she finally asked.

"No reason why he should."

Strange. Jasmine's smile wobbled a bit when she said, "Okay then. Let me get changed, and we'll meet you out in the yard in ten."

Ashley walked Jasmine partway back to her room. "Are you okay?"

"Yeah. Everything's great. I love this place. And I love that everyone here seems so in love." She gave Ash a meaningful smile. "It's an auspicious location for a wedding, don't you think?"

"Yeah. I do." Ash swallowed thickly. "Umm, I'll see you in a few minutes?"

"Absolutely."

Ashley returned to the empty dining room and retrieved her camera that sat beside her plate. She took a few pictures of the great room, a couple from the picture window on the west side. Beautiful. Wandering into the kitchen, she paused. Dillon and Gloria were there, talking quietly, and because they didn't acknowledge her, she figured they hadn't heard her come in.

Ash was about to leave but something stopped her.

Gloria was standing by the sink, the morning sun shining in and making her red curls look like a halo. Dillon was kneeling in front of her, his big hands on her belly.

"You sure it's nothing serious?"

"It's normal. They call them Braxton Hicks contractions. It's just my body's way of practicing for the real thing, apparently."

"You going to make it until after the wedding?" Dillon asked, as he leaned close, putting an ear to her belly.

"You know I will. Our baby is not coming until after Dad is married. We have an agreement, her and I."

"You mean you and him."

Ash took a picture, focused and took another, and another. She knew she had a winner, when Dillon pressed his lips to the front of Gloria's shirt, and Gloria gazed down at him like she was the goddess of love.

Quietly, she tiptoed out of the kitchen, not wanting to let the couple know that she'd been there and interrupted their poignant moment. As she made her way outside to meet up with everyone, a strange sense of melancholy overran her earlier playful, sexy thoughts.

Catching sight of Colton standing by the quads, watching her approach, made her tummy tumble. Why? It wasn't like she wanted what Dillon and Gloria had. Well, not with Colton, anyway. But that didn't change the fact that she wanted to be loved. Someday.

DESPITE THE FACT he'd only had about five hours of sleep, Colton did not feel tired. Nope. He was energized, and watching Ashley work energized him even more.

Who would have guessed she was such a wildcat?

Jesus.

He could not get enough of her. That striptease last night? That was about the hottest thing he'd ever experienced. Until she woke him up in the middle of the night, sliding her lithe body over his, kissing him and touching him, rousing him from sleep until he was wild with need.

That's what she did to him. She turned him into a feral beast.

A beast who wanted her. Now.

Unfortunately, he'd have to wait because they weren't alone. The four of them had taken the quads around to the other side of the pond where there was a nice wooden bench carved out of a fallen log.

"This is pretty," Jasmine said, running a hand along the bench before sitting down.

Ash focused on her, taking a couple of shots. "Curtis,

why don't you sit beside her so I can get two people in the shot," she said. "It will give Jasmine a better idea of how it'll look."

"I'm not one for pictures," Curtis said gruffly, looking to Colt for help.

Colt ignored the other ranch hand.

"Come on, sit," Jasmine said. "I won't bite."

Reluctantly, Curtis sat, and Ash took a few pics of them on the bench before instructing them to go down by the pond.

Colton watched it all from a distance, admiring the way Ashley used the camera as if it was an extension of herself. There were no long waits in between shots, no stupid comments like, "say cheese." She talked and moved and took pictures as natural as anything.

Colton took them up to the Doghouse next, the old homestead that overlooked the whole valley and ranch. It'd been fixed up in recent years, and now there was a rustic old log swing on the porch.

For all Jasmine spoke, Curtis stayed quiet, posing awkwardly alongside her in all the shots while Ashley worked. Colt had to admit, there was something incredibly sexy about watching Ash do her job. Witnessing her passion in action. She talked her way through poses, but she took a lot of shots when people weren't looking.

A couple times he even caught her taking sneaky pictures of him.

"Can we come back up here later?" she asked him. "This would be a great place to take some sunset pictures with the ranch down below."

"Whatever you say, boss."

Damn. Why did it satisfy him so much to see her blush? Who knew.

The next stop was the swimming hole on the edge of the property near Quarry Road. Abandoned as a quarry more than fifty years ago, the place became popular with generations of town kids as a place to hang out. It was a pretty spot; the water was a blue/green color, so clear you could see all the way down to the bottom, and surrounded by big trees on the west side. Jasmine sat on an old tire swing, which had been there even when he was a kid, while Curtis pushed and Ash took pictures.

Colton had been sitting on a log apart from the others, chewing on a blade of grass and thinking random thoughts, about what work needed doing this afternoon, about Ashley taking her clothes off, about the upcoming qualifying rodeo in Wyoming, about Ashley kissing her way down his chest…

When he heard the snap of a twig off to his right. "Whatcha doing?" he asked, catching her.

"Nothing." She smiled.

"Why don't you come sit for a bit?"

"Jasmine wants to see some more spots."

"You sure? Because she's looking pretty content exactly where she is." Colton glanced back to where Jasmine was laughing with Curtis. He didn't think he'd ever heard Curtis laugh before.

"You think she likes him?" Ashley asked.

"Dunno."

"But she's engaged."

With an exaggerated shrug, he said, "Don't ask me. I'm no good at commitment or relationships, Ash. I've never understood it."

She frowned and looked at her camera screen. Was she avoiding his gaze or scrolling through images to see if there was any evidence of his suggestion.

Nudging her with his elbow, he said, "So, what's on the agenda for tonight?"

She ignored his comment for a moment before raising

her gaze. "What on earth do you mean?" Her expression was completely deadpan.

"Well, now…" Placing his hand on her bare thigh, he made little curlicues with his fingertip. "I'm just thinking… I've gone to a whole slew of trouble, taking the morning off, carting you two around." He leaned over and nudged her shoulder with his jaw. "Touching you." He took a deep breath from that sweet spot on her neck below her ear. "Sniffing you." Placing a soft kiss on her shoulder, he whispered, "Kissing you. It's been tough work. Torture, really."

Through it all she sat perfectly still. "You've sure had it rough," she said quietly.

He couldn't read her. Was she mad at him for some reason?

Colton took hold of her chin and turned her toward him, saying, "Everything okay?"

A slow smile crept across her features, and her brown-gold eyes twinkled with sexy mischief. Her hand settled on his thigh, snaking up to settle over his crotch. "If you think this is torture—" she squeezed, gently "—then you haven't seen anything yet."

It had been a pretty much perfect day. The weather was warm but not too warm. The air smelled of fresh grass and blossoms from the rain, the trees had that bright green spring hue, and the pond had sparkled with the mid-morning light. Getting to spend the entire morning behind her camera taking pictures was the best, and she knew she had some amazing shots. But perfect lighting aside, it helped that she got to do her favorite thing after a night of extreme pleasure. Then there was tonight and the promise of even more pleasure.

Except that somehow she had to come up with a way to torture Colton. She drummed her nails on the tabletop, while she waited for the images from her camera to transfer to her computer.

After they'd returned from their outing, Jasmine had gone to her room to make calls to her parents and Parker. She returned just as Ashley was sorting through the images.

"Wow," Jazz said when Ash clicked on the photo of Dillon and Gloria in the kitchen. "Seriously, Ash. That is an amazing photo." She touched the screen. "Is that the natural light or did you enhance it? Because it's—oh, my God, perfect—like they're surrounded by the white light of love."

"I know. Right?" Ash said, gazing at the image. Something hot formed at the back of her throat. "I haven't done a thing to it, but it's easy to take a good picture when people don't know you're doing it." She smiled up at Jasmine. "It also helps when both parties are so completely photogenic." She closed the image and opened a file with the series of pictures of Jasmine. "Kind of like you."

Jazz made a derisive noise and waved off the comment. But she leaned forward as Ash went through each image individually. Jasmine and Curtis sitting on the bench, looking awkward. Jazz and Curtis sitting in the grass by the pond, talking shyly. The two of them sitting on the porch of the old homestead, staring off into the distance. Curtis pushing Jazz on the tire swing over the swimming hole, laughing…

"They're really good," Jasmine said slowly.

They were good. Maybe a little too good. Whereas the photo of Dillon and Gloria was about love, this series seemed to chronicle the story of a budding attraction. A cowboy showing a city girl a good time.

"Do you think Parker will like them?" Ash asked hesitantly.

"I don't know." She paused. "Honestly? I don't think

he cares. He told me to go ahead and plan the whole wedding because he says couples just fight when they both try to get involved."

"Hmm." Ash focused on the screen as she created folders and dropped the images into the appropriate ones. "Do you have a favorite location out of any of these?"

Jazz stared at the computer screen. "I like them all but…"

"But what?"

"I think the swimming hole is my favorite."

Ashley found the series of pictures and opened them up again. "It is really picturesque. You two look like you're having fun. What were you laughing about?"

Jasmine's cheeks turned pink as she grinned secretively at Ash. "Do you remember playing dice?"

Ash remembered the game but had never played it. It was meant for a group of young singles to play while drinking.

"Curtis reminded me of a time I coerced him into playing."

"I didn't know that."

"I didn't always tell you everything." She got a defensive look in her eye.

"Like?"

"Like the fact that I'd always kind of liked him. He was so different than the other guys—quiet and stoic." She met Ashley's gaze. "Kind of like a male version of you."

"So, when I told you *I* liked him in high school?"

Jasmine blinked, then blurted, "I told him you didn't. Then I seduced him. On purpose."

It didn't matter that all of this was old news. It was like Jasmine had just stabbed her right in the gut. Her best friend. "Why would you do that?"

"Don't you know?"

"No."

"I was so jealous of you."

"Of me?" Ash pressed a hand to her breast, incredulous. "Why on earth would you be jealous of me?"

"Why wouldn't I be?" She paced around the table. "You have always known *exactly* who you are, what you want. You don't do stuff to impress people or to please them. You're just you, and you don't apologize for it."

Ash blinked in confused. "But…"

"Come on. You must have known how jealous I was." She glanced at the computer. There was an image of Colton sitting on a log by the swimming hole, a long blade of grass hanging out one side of his mouth. A thoughtful expression on his handsome features. "How jealous I still am."

"What could you possibly be jealous about?"

"You and Colton." She pointed to the screen. "You two are so hot for each other. It's crazy making."

Oh, shit.

The truth sat at the back of Ashley's throat, burning her esophagus and sending liquid fire down into the pit of her stomach.

"I want what you have, Ash."

Ashley opened her mouth, willing the truth to fall out, but the words wouldn't come. They were stuck, seared into the back of her throat. Jasmine had just confessed something that couldn't have been easy. Etiquette dictated that she should come clean, too.

So, why couldn't she?

Because the minute you confess, it will all be over between you and Colton. Admit it, Ash, you don't want it to end.

13

ALL DURING CHORES, Colton could not stop thinking about what Ashley had in mind for tonight, his mind wandering to all kinds of wonderful forms of torture during the long silences that stretched between him and Curtis. The man was typically quiet, but today he was mute, not saying a word the entire time they were out in the pasture fixing fences. He made a few grumbling comments when they checked the herd and the calves, and he may have strung all of four words together when they were setting out fresh salt licks.

Back at the barn, he went all silent again, giving Colton ample time to fantasize about Ashley.

Because they'd taken the morning off, they didn't finish chores until well after dinnertime, and by the time he returned, Ashley was waiting for him in the bunkhouse surrounded by the most delicious aroma of something cooking in his apartment-sized oven.

Just seeing her there, sitting on his couch, making herself at home in his space did something to him. Surprisingly, it wasn't a *bad* something, which was normally the case when females became too comfortable at his place: leaving their shit lying around, rearranging his stuff, that kind of thing.

This was completely different.

He hung up his hat on the peg by the door and tugged

off his dirty boots. "I need a shower," he said by way of a greeting.

Without lifting her head from the magazine she was reading, she said, "Okay."

He waited for her to look up. When she didn't he said, "You want to come help?"

She slowly raised her gaze. "Nope."

"Any reason why not?"

She plucked at the front of her shirt and sniffed. "I'm already clean."

"It's not about getting clean, Ash."

She raised a brow at this comment. "Oh, I know that." Then went right back to reading her magazine.

When he didn't move, she eventually looked up again. "What?"

"You playing hard to get?"

"No."

"Because I'm of half a mind to come over there, scoop you up and carry you off to the shower like some damn caveman."

Her lips twisted with a hidden smile. "Someone needs to be here to take the chicken out of the oven in a few minutes."

"You made me roast chicken?"

"I might have."

"Mashed potatoes?"

"Yep." There was no inflection in her voice whatsoever though her pretty lips twitched in a very kissable way.

"Gravy and string beans?"

Her reply was nothing more than her flipping the page of the magazine and sighing heavily as if all these questions were a burden. But Colton knew better. It was no coincidence she'd made his all-time favorite meal. She must have asked Dillon.

Now why would she go and do that?

He didn't know, but he was sporting a grin as he ambled on through to the bathroom. Sporting more than a grin, which was evident after undressing. He stepped beneath the spray of the shower, Ashley's voice saying softly in his ear, *If you think this is torture, then you haven't seen anything yet.*

Colton had never looked forward to a meal more, not only because it smelled so damn good but because of what Ashley had in store for dessert.

Sweet torture, he hoped. Maybe with some whipped cream as a garnish.

Of course, he wouldn't let her tease him very long. Oh, no. Tormenting her until she screamed his name was just way too much fun. Spending any time with the woman was just way too much fun.

By the time he was dressed and shaved, the food was on the table. He sat down and helped himself to a mess of it, piling it high.

"I'll take this as payment any day of the week," he said with his mouth full, indicating the meal with a wave of his fork.

Ashley smiled as she helped herself to food.

"I didn't know you cooked."

"Yeah, well…after my mom died, we all took turns in the kitchen. Then when Beth got married, followed closely by Zoe and Chloe, it was just me and Brandi around to cook for my dad."

Colton forked another mouthful and chewed thoughtfully. "When did your mom die?"

"When I was five."

"No wonder you were always such a quiet, serious kid."

She made a noise while eating. Once she swallowed she said, "As if you remember me from when we were kids."

"Sure I do. You were a little thing, quiet as a mouse." He drank deeply before adding, "I spit in your hair once."

Her eyes went wide.

"It took me a while to remember because you don't look much like that little girl anymore."

Ashley coughed and then took a long drink of water.

"You okay?"

She cleared her throat. "Yep." And then kept eating.

"You're not still upset about the spitting incident, are you? Boys go through weird phases. I don't know what it is about spitting."

She shook her head.

Huh. She was either being mysterious or she was quiet for some other reason.

Well, he was just going to have to find out, wasn't he?

He nudged her leg with his toe—his bare toe, since he hadn't bothered to put on fresh socks—and she twitched.

Then she looked up, gazing at him cooly.

"Everything okay?"

She nodded quickly and then went back to eating.

He let his toe linger on her lower leg and then slowly drew it up, past her knee and thigh, until his foot rested on the edge of the chair between her legs. She set her fork down and blinked at him from across the little table.

Without a word, she eased her pelvis forward in her seat so that his foot was right at the juncture between her legs. It was Ashley who raised and lowered her pelvis against the bottom of his foot, wriggling her warm self against him. Lord help him, he could feel her heat right through the denim.

He rubbed right back.

Her lids opened and closed lazily as she scooped a forkful of potatoes into her mouth and slowly ate while he used his foot to do wicked things to her.

"You like that?" he asked, his voice gruff.

"The potatoes?"

"Sure."

"Mmm-hmm. Yep."

He helped himself to a mouthful of potatoes, too—nice and creamy and buttery—while he wriggled his foot along the seam of her jeans. "Best I've ever had."

"I find that hard to believe."

"Doesn't make it any less true."

She set her fork down before reaching beneath the table and grabbing his foot. "You're pretty good at the sweet talk, aren't you?"

"I don't know what that means."

"Oh, I think you do." She skimmed her short nails up the bottom of his foot; an acute ticklish sensation had him jerking his leg and nearly toppling the entire table.

With a laugh she pushed his foot off her lap and stood. "Finish up. I want to head back up to the Doghouse to take some sunset pictures."

She gathered up dirty plates and carried them to the little kitchen all calm and cool as if he hadn't just been grinding his bare foot against her pussy. He picked up the platter of chicken and followed her, trapping her in the small kitchenette.

"Do you have any idea how unfair that was?" He set the platter on the counter and rested his hands on her slim hips, pulling her against him so that she could feel him.

She smiled sweetly. "I warned you."

He leaned down. "Yes, you did," he whispered. "But I'm willing to bet that you came first." He blew gently in her ear. "And—" he touched the lobe of her ear with his tongue "—I'm going to make you feel so fucking good, you're going to beg me to make you come a second time."

Though her gaze was aloof, her soft pants gave her away.

"You think you're the shit, don't you?"

"It's not my fault," he said, dipping his fingers down

the front of her shirt, grazing the top of her breasts, "that you can't get enough of me."

She took hold of his hand and pulled it out of her shirt. Her cheeks were flushed, her eyes bright, her lips plump like they'd been kissing.

"The fact that you're practically bursting out of your jeans means you can't get enough of me." She held her hand out for him to take. "So, I'll take that bet. Let's see who makes who come first."

Ash wrapped her arms around Colton's waist and snugged herself right up against his broad back as they made their way by quad back up to the old homestead. The evening was cool, and it was nice to be so close to Colt. He was so solid and warm and strong. Capable, too. That was sexy.

He was a manly man. Ash had never given it much thought, but manly men were hot.

Yes, but it's Colton Cross we're talking about here, her snarky side reminded her. For some reason, Ash couldn't quite conjure up the old disdainful sentiments.

Once parked, Ash got to work taking pictures of the ranch down below—she planned to give the pictures to Gloria and Dillon to use on their promotional materials. Then she took some pictures of Colt when he wasn't looking: one where his hat was pulled down low, his hands were stuck in his pocket and he was looking down with the sky painted in watercolors behind him.

"Can you sit on the step?" she asked.

"Why?"

"I just want to get a few pictures."

"You don't want pictures of me."

Was he putting her on? Pretending to be modest? Maybe, except that every time he caught her taking a picture, he ruined it by putting a hand up to block her or turned around. Finally, he put his hand out for her camera.

"You know what I think?"

"No."

"I think you need to have some pictures taken of you."

"No. I'm not photogenic." She shook her head and took a couple more shots as the sun quickly descended behind the peaks. When she finished, Colton was standing there with his hand extended.

"Give it to me."

"No."

"Do you really want to do this?"

"Do what?"

He didn't answer. Instead, he grabbed her about the waist, pinning both arms down with one of his ridiculously strong limbs and wrestling the strap of her camera from around her neck.

"Hey!"

"How many times do I have to teach you about messing with me?" Colton asked, taking a bunch of pictures, not bothering to focus. Ashley grabbed for the camera, but he hefted it out of her range and kept depressing the shutter even though he wasn't looking through the viewfinder.

"Stop!"

"Nope. We need some pics of the photographer." Holding the camera aloft, he simply held the shutter down. There had to be at least one good one in the dozens of images he was taking.

"Enough." She finally plopped down on the porch swing, and Colt sat beside her, handing her the camera. She left it on her lap, and the two of them sat there, gently swinging in silence for a few minutes as dusk settled around them.

"You're an ass," Ash finally said.

"Maybe. But you love it."

She elbowed him and then secured the lens cap over her camera. "So," she said, "what's this place used for?" She glanced up at him. "And why is it called the Doghouse?"

Colt explained how it was the original homestead and that after the Wells family, the original owners of the ranch, had built down in the valley, it was used for the men of the family when they were in trouble.

She laughed.

"The Wells men made a point of getting into trouble. Often. Then they'd come up here, not out of penitence but to host poker games. All the men and ranch hands from around these parts would come out."

"Really?"

"Yep. Even my brothers used to come here when they were teenagers to play poker and drink whiskey."

"Cool."

"Yeah." Colton stared off into the distance. "God. I looked up to them so much, I wanted to be just like them. Lots of times I feel like I missed out on stuff after my oldest brother died."

"That was when you moved, right?"

"Yep. Sold the ranch and just me and my parents went to Arizona."

"But you used to come back in the summers, didn't you?"

"Yep. Worked right here, on this ranch." He nudged her. "How come you remember me from those days, but I don't remember you?"

Ashley shrugged. "Because I'm invisible." She hadn't meant to say it out loud, it just came out.

Colt caught a fine wisp of hair as it fluttered across her face and tucked it behind her ear. "Why did you want to be invisible?"

She covered his hand. "It wasn't a choice."

"Sure it is." He ran the backs of his knuckles down her cheek. "Believe me, Ash, you have no problem standing out when you want to."

She drew her brows together. Was that true? Had she purposefully flown under the radar for most of her life? If so, why?

"Or, maybe I didn't remember you because I have a one-track mind—"

"A truer statement has never been told," Ash interjected, eyeing the fly of his jeans.

He chuckled. "Believe it or not, I was focused on emulating my big brother. That's when Dillon made the pro tour, and I knew that's what I was going to do, too." His face turned serious as a faraway look came into his eyes. "It's going to happen this year, Ash. I got enough points on the amateur tour last year to be invited to a pro qualifying event in Wyoming in a couple of weeks. I'm going to make the pros, and then things will change."

"How so?"

"The pro tour runs all year. New towns every weekend. Not just little shit holes but big cities. Then there's the money you can win. Big pots. More than enough to live on." He shut his eyes. "It's only been my dream since I was a kid." He glanced at the door behind him. "And used to try to follow my brothers here."

Ashley stared off into the distance, too, trying hard *not* to think about Colton in all those different places with all those adoring women, but she couldn't. The thought made her chest ache.

Time to think about something else.

Ash gazed up at the old house. "You have a key to this place?"

"No, but I know where one's hiding. Why?"

"I think it's time you played poker at the Doghouse."

COLTON HAD NEVER spent much time up at the old homestead. The inside was rustic, a fireplace on one end with a love seat and a well-worn chair. In another corner was one of those old wood-burning ovens surrounded by cupboards. There was a small table with a couple of chairs, some shelves filled with old tins, lanterns and other odds and ends.

"How can there be no cards here?" Ashley asked as she went through the drawers and cupboards he'd just been through. Cutlery. Dusty cups and dishes. An old tea tin and biscuits circa the last century. No cards.

"Don't ask me," Colt said, finding a bottle of whiskey stashed at the back of one cupboard and plopping it on the table. "But at least there's this."

There was a drawer at one end of the table, and Ashley pulled it open. She reached inside and fished something out, shaking whatever it was in her hands. "You ever played dice?" she asked.

"Like craps?"

"No. It's like truth or dare with dice. If the two numbers add up to an even number you have to tell a truth. Odd, it's a dare. If you roll a one—" she pointed to the whiskey "—you take a shot. And sixes—"

"Sixes mean you have to take off an article of clothing," Colton finished for her.

Her secret, sexy smile appeared at that comment. "So you have played."

He shook his head. "Nope. Never played."

"That surprises me."

"Well, the point was to hook up with girls you liked. I never needed to play." He bit down on his lower lip to hide his grin.

Ashley rolled her eyes at this. "God, you're full of yourself. Just when I think you might be a decent guy, you remind me of your arrogance."

"Arrogance."

"Yep."

"Is it arrogance that makes you come so hard your eyes roll right up inside your head?"

She punched him.

"Ouch."

"And you're an ass. Are we going to play, or are you just going to continue being your conceited self?"

He pulled a chair out for her and waved dramatically for her to sit, pushing it in like a gentleman—which he had no intention of being from here on in—before sitting himself.

"You found them, you start," he said.

Ashley shook the dice and rolled a one and a two. Colton passed her the open bottle of whiskey. "Drink."

Without cringing, she took a swig right from the bottle, wiped her lips with the back of her hand and set the bottle down. "Your turn."

Colton rolled a six and a four.

"Take off your shirt," she said without hesitation.

"Why don't you take it off for me?" Colton asked, though he started in on the buttons, not expecting her to take him up on his offer.

"Okay. Come here."

He got up and went to stand right in front of her. Starting from where he'd left off, she slowly popped each one, dragging her fingernails down the center of his chest as she went.

"Can't keep your hands off me, I see." His voice was rough around the edges, probably because her hands were now lingering low on his abdomen, making his stomach muscles contract.

"You have a nice body." She spread his shirt wide and gave him a good once-over. "It's too bad you're so very well aware of that fact." She fished down beneath the waistband of his jeans, but his belt didn't allow her to get very far.

With effort, he moved away from her touch and sat down again. "Your turn."

14

How LONG HAD they been playing? It was hard to tell, but she was down to her panties and bra, and Colt was down to his underwear. She'd had four—no, five—shots of whiskey and had confessed who her first crush had ever been.

Of course she'd lied, saying it was Curtis, which was enough of a surprise to Colton. No way she'd ever tell him that she'd had a crush on him in grade school. God. That was just way too embarrassing.

When Colton had rolled an odd number, she'd dared him to eat one of the ancient biscuits, which he only choked down by chasing it with big gulps of whiskey. His ruddy cheeks were flushed, and his eyes were bright, and she wondered if he was starting to feel the warm effects of the whiskey, too?

On her next roll, she got a two and a three.

"Dare, huh?" Colton studied her, with a wicked gleam in his eyes. He tapped his lips as he contemplated what he was going to make her do. He got up and took a peek out of the window. It was dark now. "I dare you to streak around the Doghouse."

"But I'm still dressed."

"Well, then, you're going to have to get naked, lady," he said in a deep, commanding voice.

Was it wrong that she liked him when he was bossy like that?

Nah. As long as he never told anyone.

Slowly Ash stood, turned and then unclasped her bra while her back was to him. After shimmying out of her panties, she ran for the door, and out she went.

The cool night air caressed her naked body in strange and wonderful ways as she sprinted around the old homestead, giddy as a schoolgirl after sneaking her first drink.

When she got back to the porch and went to open the door, it was locked. What the...

She pounded. "Colton, let me in." She glanced over her shoulder, scouring the dark landscape, hoping for no signs of life. "Colton!" Using her closed fist, she pounded three more times before hearing the latch on the door slide. Because the light was behind him when Colt opened the door she couldn't see his expression, but she could guess.

"What's the problem?"

Ash elbowed him in the gut as she pushed past. Though the truth was, she wasn't angry. Not even when Colton held on to her arms to keep her from going by. He shut the door with his foot and let his gaze rake over her.

"Hey," she said, trying to cover herself up.

"Why are you so damn shy sometimes?" Catching her hands, he pulled her arms away so he could take a nice long look at her. "It's not like I haven't seen you closer than this." His gaze lingered before he finally released her.

She snatched her bra and panties from the floor and put them back on.

"You've got a very nice body," he said, repeating what she'd said to him. "Too bad you don't know it."

She glared at him over her shoulder. Except she wasn't mad. Not at all. In fact, being with Colton made her feel... sexy. With him, she wanted to flaunt her body because she loved the look of desire that came into his eyes when he gazed at her.

No one had ever looked at her like that. Not even the Spaniard.

Once dressed again, they sat back at the table, and Colton rolled the dice. One of his rolls was a one, and he took a long pull from the whiskey bottle and then passed the dice.

Next Ashley rolled a four and a two. "Truth," she said. She drummed her fingers on the table waiting for him to ask her a question.

"Tell me, Ashley," he said quietly, pulling his chair so close their bare knees were touching. "Have you ever been in love?"

This was not the question she'd expected. She sat up straight and blinked. "In love?"

"Yes."

Slowly, she shook her head from side to side. "No. You?"

"Nope."

"Well, that's one thing we have in common."

"That's not the only thing we have in common." He hooked his feet around the legs of her chair and pulled her close. With his hands on her knees, he spread them so that his legs could fit between. Up his hands went. Sliding slowly up, and up.

And up.

"Tell me something else," he prodded.

"What?" She choked on the word because his thumbs had met at the crotch of her panties, and together pressed into her damp heat.

"Why are we doing this?"

She leaned toward him, hands on his legs, resting her head on his lovely chest. "Um, because it feels good?"

"True." His thumbs worked beneath the elastic of her panties, dipping into her as his fingers kneaded her thighs.

She groaned, leaned forward and bit him.

"I'm just thinking…" Colton began.

Ash stopped listening. What he was doing to her felt so damn good, she couldn't concentrate on words when her mind had gone blank from pleasure. With hands on his shoulders, she pushed herself to her feet, wriggled out of her panties and climbed right up onto Colton's lap, straddling him. Holding on to the sides of his face, she kissed him.

"Did you hear me?" he asked against her mouth.

"No."

He licked across her lips and then whispered, "Why not keep doing what we're doing?"

"Good plan." She ground her bare pussy against his boxers. Oh, sweet mercy, he was hard. "Now be quiet so we can keep doing what we're doing."

Colton held her hips steady and leaned back to look at her. "I don't think you're hearing me."

Despite his firm grasp on her hips, Ash swiveled over his erection. "Oh, I'm hearing you." She reached a hand between them and fondled him. "So you can stop talking now." She wrapped a hand around his neck and pulled him to her.

With a groan, Colton thrust up with his pelvis while his tongue took ownership of her mouth. "You're the boss."

So not true. Even this kiss felt different. It felt…possessive and domineering, like Colton owned her or something.

Strangely, she liked it.

A lot.

It was late, and they were back at the bunkhouse lying in bed. Good thing he'd eaten a big supper.

"What are you chuckling about?" Ashley asked as she rolled up onto his chest.

"Just glad you cooked a hearty meal." He grabbed her

ass. "Because you might be just a little thing, but you take a lot of stamina."

She nestled against him, laughing softly. Good Lord. Colt couldn't remember feeling so satisfied before. Not one to forget a bet, he'd made sure Ash orgasmed well before he did. Then in typical Ashley form, she made sure he came again, too.

They'd been having so much fun he'd completely lost track of time. With a groan, he reached across Ashley to the nightstand and picked up his cell. She stopped him from looking by grabbing the phone away.

"It's late. That's all you need to know."

"Some of us have to get up early around here."

"I do, too," she said, poking him in the chest.

"Where are you off to?"

"I've got to drive back to town to work a shift at the flower shop tomorrow and then again the next day."

Wrapping his arms around her, he said, "You leaving me already?"

"A girl's gotta make a living. Another couple months and I'll have saved up enough to get out of Dodge."

"Where you going to go?"

"Anywhere but here."

"What's wrong with here?"

"Nothing...exactly." Her voice trailed off. "I just want to make it on my own, you know?" Drawing circles on his chest, she continued. "I want to see places. Meet new people. Experience things."

"So you want to travel? Where would you go? What would you do?"

She was quiet so long, he thought she might have fallen asleep. When she finally answered, it was in a soft, uncertain voice. "I have this plan."

"Yes?"

"It's... Well, I've never told anyone, but..."

"But?"

"I want to travel around America and find the best places in the country that no one's ever heard of. I'm going to photo blog about it."

"That sounds...awesome."

She lay still for a second. "Do you want to see? I mean, it's okay if you don't, but I've already started up the site, and I don't have many followers, but I figured I might as well get started now, right?"

"I'd love to see."

Ash arched her sweet little body in order to reach her phone on the nightstand. She tapped on it for a few seconds before turning it around and showing him.

America's Best Kept Secrets—A Photo Blog.

Holy shit. Her pictures weren't just good. They were... amazing. The lighting, the composition. He wasn't much for art, but he could tell the difference between just a good picture any Joe Blow could take and one taken by a professional. Ash was a professional. She'd blogged about the county fair, saying it was a jewel of the West. Blogged about the guest ranch and had used some of the images from their outing, although none of the people were identifiable. He scrolled down and saw the nearby ghost town, Silverton. She must have taken pictures early in the morning after a rain because steam rose up from the ground as if it was spirits from the deserted place.

"Wow, Ash. This is really good. You are so talented."

She shifted in his arms. "Do you really think so?"

"Yeah. I'm blown away." Colton played with the soft hair on the side of her head, realizing how much talent was packed away in this little package lying so snug within his arms.

He felt proud of her, he really did. But he'd be lying if there wasn't another part of him that didn't like the idea of Ashley being out in the world blogging and having "experiences" without him. It was a totally stupid, irrational feeling because, on the other hand, he had the same desire: to go out and ride and have his own experiences without being tied down. Oh, yeah. There was nothing better than moving from town to town, meeting new people and connecting with old friends.

But he'd kind of figured that at the end of the day if he ever came back to Half Moon Creek, Ashley would be here.

That made him a selfish ass, didn't it?

Well, it's not like he was about to articulate those feelings.

Instead, he snuggled his gifted little photographer up nice and close. "You're very good," he whispered. "Have I told you that?"

"Not recently," she purred.

He tugged on the blanket, exposing her breast. "You are." He circled her breast, drawing smaller and smaller circles until he reached her nipple. "Very, very good…" He gently pinched, squeezing her nipple between his fingers.

"And you," she groaned, "are very, very bad."

He rolled her over so he was on top and kissed her tight bud. "That's about right." He clamped on with his teeth gently before releasing to say, "And I'm not above corrupting you."

"You wouldn't dare." Her legs twined languidly between his as she opened her thighs.

"I would." He bit her other nipple. "And the best part is, you're going to love it."

IT WAS LATE afternoon, and Ashley was at the flower shop for her second shift of the week. She'd already finished all the orders and had them boxed in the fridge and ready to go for tomorrow's delivery. She'd swept and tidied behind the counter. The work was done for now, so she grabbed her cell and tapped in her password, opening up her message app and rereading some of the texts she'd shared with Colton over the last forty-eight hours.

No, not texts. Sexts.

You ever been tied up before?

No. You?

I don't kiss and tell.

Maybe not, but you sure as hell moan a lot when you're kissing.

I think someone is getting confused about who's doing the moaning.

Maybe it's been too long and your memory's failing.

It has definitely been too long and we are rectifying that tonight...

The bell rang over the shop door, and Ashley closed her message app before looking up.

"Jasmine!" Ashley checked the clock on the wall. "You're early."

"I know. I hope it's no inconvenience." Her face was flushed, like she'd been out in the sun too long.

"No. Not at all." Ashley grabbed the stack of wedding arrangement catalogs and carried them over to the table where the two of them could sit to go through them. "How are things going at the ranch? Did you choose a menu?"

"Um, I think so."

Hmm. Jasmine replied sans her usual enthusiasm.

"Okay, well, let's see if we can choose some flowers."

Ash opened the first catalog. "We can pretty much re-create anything that's in here. Do you have any favorite flowers?"

"I've always liked lilies," Jasmine said softly as she flipped through the first few pages without seeming to be really looking at the arrangements.

"Have you chosen your colors?"

"No."

Ashley's message app beeped. It was Colton.

When's your break? I'm in town and I'm horny.

Afraid of the snort that was sneaking up the back of her throat, Ash pinched her nostrils before it could escape and switched her phone to vibrate. Pretending to be interested in the images Jasmine was looking at, she pointed to one arrangement. "That one's nice."

"Mmm. It's okay." That was her only comment before flipping the page.

With her phone in her lap, Ashley quickly typed back, I'll be off in a couple of hours. You seriously need to learn some patience.

Overrated. Isn't there a backroom in that shop?

Colton!

Simple question.

Ash was just about to respond when Jasmine shut the book with a slam and then, with elbows on the table, dropped her face to her hands.

"Jazz? What's wrong?"

With a faraway voice, maybe because her head was pointing down, she said, "Curtis kissed me."

"Bellamy?"

Jasmine raised her head. Her expression said, "Is there any other?"

"Okay," Ash said slowly. A sudden, troubling thought occurred to Ashley. "Did Curtis force himself on you?"

"No." Jasmine shook her head. "He didn't force himself on me." She rubbed her temples.

"So, who kissed who?"

"It was mostly me. At first."

"Why would you do that?"

"He's a really good kisser."

"Jasmine!"

She sighed. "We may have groped a bit, too."

"Groped? What? Why?"

"I don't know." She met Ashley's eyes and looked away.

"Are you…in love with him?"

"No-oo." Jasmine drew the word out. "I mean, I still have fond feelings, you know."

Yes. Ash did know. As stupid as it was, she'd never quite forgotten Colton or forgiven him for the spitting incident. She supposed it would have been even harder to forget if they'd been older and had actually kissed before he moved away.

"It doesn't mean anything. It's nostalgia."

"So, what are you going to do? Call off the wedding?"

"No. God, no." Jasmine got a wild look in her eye. "It's not that big a deal, is it?"

Tilting her head to one side, Ash studied her friend. Jasmine was staring at a point just past Ashley's shoulder while absently twisting her engagement ring round and round and round.

"Are you going to tell Parker?"

Shaking her head, Jasmine said, "I don't think so. I mean, what for? It was just a kiss, with a teensy bit of groping. It's normal, right? Pre-wedding jitters and all that?"

"Yeah," Ash said slowly. "I guess so."

After a heavy sigh, Jazz said, "I've been away too long."

"Maybe."

With large, luminous eyes, like they might overspill with tears at any moment, Jasmine said, "I think part of the reason I did it is because..." She faltered as her gaze flicked toward the door where the bell had just chimed.

"Hi, Colton," Jasmine called with extra enthusiasm.

"Hey, Jazz."

He strode into the shop, came right up to where Ash was sitting and hugged her from behind, bending down to nuzzle her neck. "Hey, babe."

"Hey, yourself." God, having Colton's arms around her felt so wonderful. Stranger still, it felt totally natural.

Jazz cleared her throat. "I'm glad you're here, Colton," she said. "I was just telling Ashley that I'm needed back in Chicago."

"What?" Ashley blurted, shrugging out from beneath Colton's arms to stand. "You're heading back?"

"Yeah. That's why I came in early. Stopping in to say goodbye on my way to Butte." She glanced at her phone, checking the time. "In fact, I've got to run. I'm booked on the next flight out this evening." Jazz gave her a tight smile before turning to Colton with arms open wide. No handshakes for Jazz, it was a hug or nothing, no matter how emotionally distressed she was.

Colton gave her a quick hug and let go, but Jasmine kept holding on. Once she finally released him she turned to Ash, hugging her hard and whispering, "Please, don't say anything about what I told you."

"Of course not."

She pulled back. "And you have to come visit me. We'll choose colors and dresses and flowers and everything then, okay?"

Still completely surprised by what had all just transpired, Ash simply nodded.

Smiling a wide, wobbly smile, Jasmine said, "It was so great to catch up, Ash. We'll be in touch." Turning to Colt she said, "And so nice to meet you. I sure hope you'll be around this summer for my wedding."

Colton's gaze flicked to Ash for a nanosecond. His brows drawn together in a question. "Yeah, me, too."

15

THE CHIMES OVER the door jingled after Jasmine departed.

"Everything okay?" Colton asked.

"I think so." Though the wrinkle between her brows indicated otherwise. She smiled tightly and waved to Jasmine who'd stopped in the shop window to blow kisses before settling her sunglasses over her face and walking away.

Ash's gaze moved from the window to him. "So...Jasmine's gone."

"It appears so."

"I guess that's it, then." She indicated the space between them with a flick of her hand. "We're officially done."

Colton frowned. "Done?"

"Yeah. No reason to pretend anymore."

"But I thought we'd agreed..."

"We agreed it would end when Jasmine left," Ash interrupted.

"Just like that?"

She shrugged, as if it didn't matter one way or the other. "Yeah, just like that." She stuck her hand out as if she wanted him to take it and shake it. The close of a business deal.

He took her hand but didn't shake it; he held it, caressing the underside of her wrist. "There's her wedding this summer and—"

"Which you won't be here for, right?" She tugged her hand out of his grasp. "You'll be on the road?"

Colton chewed the inside of his cheek. "Yeah, but I could come back for it."

Ashley crossed her arms over her chest. "Why would you do that?"

He touched her cheek. "Why do you think?"

She flinched away from his touch. "I don't need any more fake dates, Colt. I don't." She held her hands up as if to ward him off.

Colton frowned. "You think I faked everything?"

She laughed. A bitter, cynical sound. "I think you like sex, and you'll take it however you can get it."

"Are you serious?" Shit. The old Ashley from the Prospectors was back. Cutting and ornery and treating him like he was a jerk for no apparent reason. "And our agreement?" He was thinking about what he'd said in the Doghouse, about wanting to keep doing what they were doing because it felt so good.

"It's done." She looked out the window. "I'm forever indebted, okay? But now…" Her voice broke, and she coughed to cover it up. "We need to go our separate ways." She waved toward the door. "Goodbye, Colt."

Colton wanted to argue, but the phone rang and Ashley picked it up to answer, turning away from him as if he was nobody.

Fine.

He turned and stalked out of the store. He'd even made it down the block to his truck when he stopped, not bothering to open the door or get in. He kicked the tire a couple of times before leaning against the side, arms crossed, thinking.

Hard to do when he was so friggin' mad.

The woman drove him crazy.

No woman had ever driven him this crazy before.

Colton pushed himself away from the truck and strode all the way back up the block to the flower shop. He pushed open the door so hard it knocked over the umbrella stand on the other side. Ashley looked up, her face pale, her pretty lips parted in shock.

"You saying you haven't had fun with me?" Colton demanded.

Whoever Ashley was speaking to on the phone, she asked them if she could call them back and gently set the phone down on the counter.

"Did you hear me?"

"Yes, I heard you," Ashley said.

"And?"

"And that's not what I'm saying."

"Are you saying you didn't like all those things we did together?"

She crossed her arms over her chest.

He leaned against the counter. "Remember how my tongue makes you fall apart? How I've got fingernail marks down my back? How you like to beg me to go faster?"

"Goddamn it, Colt," she whispered thickly.

"You like it. I like it. Why can't we just keep doing it?"

Her face clouded over. "You're leaving in a few weeks. I'm leaving at the end of the summer. There's no point."

Oh, yes, there was a fucking point, and he was going to prove it to her. He stalked around the side of the counter until he was standing right in front of her, looking down at her.

He moved closer until there was only a sliver of space between them. He wanted to reach for her, desperately, but he didn't. Instead, he propped a hand on the counter on either side of her. She had to lean so far back to avoid touching him that she was practically lying on the countertop.

"The point is, Ashley, there is some powerful chemistry between us." He wedged his knee between her legs. "Sure, maybe we discovered it by accident. Maybe neither of us planned on it. But it's there, and don't you dare try to deny it."

She drew a sharp breath in through her nose.

"I want you in my bed." He rotated his knee between her parted thighs. "And I know for a fact you want to be there, too."

She opened her mouth to speak, but no words came out, only a soft little moan.

"This will end when it's time. We both know that." He cupped the back of her head and drew her close. "But that time is not right now," he whispered against her mouth before kissing her.

The phone ringing reminded him that they were at her place of employment. Colton released her so she could answer. He waited while she took an order, running his fingers beneath her shirt along the bare skin of her lower back.

After she'd hung up the phone, she turned to him. "So, what are you suggesting? A friends-with-benefits thing until you leave?"

"I suppose that's what I'm suggesting, yeah."

"And then it's goodbye?" she asked, as if wanting to make sure he knew what was what.

"Yep. Then it's goodbye."

She shut her eyes and inhaled deeply. He just knew her mind was working behind those closed lids.

Meanwhile, her body swayed against him, leaning into his touch, melting into him in a way that felt too damn good to say goodbye.

"Okay," she said softly. "Deal." She stuck out her hand to seal it.

He took her hand and pulled it around his waist, bringing her close and kissing her soundly—a much better way to seal a deal—before heading back around the other side of the counter. Just before the door, he called, "Oh, and you're coming with me to Gloria's dad's wedding next week."

"I'm already going," she replied. "We're doing the flowers, and I'm the photographer."

"That may be, but just to be clear, you're also going with me."

BACK AT HER father's place, Ashley opened the file named CC Cowboy—a not so subtle code for Colton Cross—and scrolled through the images, all forty-seven of them. Out of them all there were three that were her absolute favorites.

The first was Colton riding across the yard, the mountains in the background, the sun shining behind him creating a halo effect around him. An angel? That so did not describe Colton, and yet the image made him appear otherworldly, like some warrior god. She opened her next favorite. This one was taken when he didn't know she was there. Colton was standing in the back of a truck, his shirtsleeves rolled up and the collar unbuttoned as he forked hay. She enlarged the image, touching her computer screen where the muscles on his arms stood out. Those strong arms had been around her last night *and* the night before. That hard body had lain naked on top of her. Had made love to her.

All those muscles were hers to touch and kiss and lick and—oh, God—she could not get enough of his body.

She skipped to the next image—which was her favorite—of Colton sitting by the swimming hole, looking off into the distance, a blade of grass in his mouth. He just looked…like a cowboy. Stoic. Thoughtful. Timeless.

In this image Colton wasn't the cocky bull rider with the mischievous grin; he was a man who had deep thoughts and complicated desires.

He was way more than Ashley had ever given him credit for.

"That's a nice shot."

Ash spun around. Brandi stood inside her room checking out the enlarged image on her computer screen. Ash snapped the laptop shut and stood up, blocking her computer as if the image was still visible. "What are you doing here?"

"Um, in case you've forgotten, I live here, too."

"Yeah, well, this is my room." God. She needed to get out of Half Moon. This was the same fight she and Brandi had been having since they'd moved into separate bedrooms in the fifth grade.

"Seriously, Ash. I was trying to compliment you. That picture of Colton is really good."

"Right."

Making a growly sound, Brandi turned to walk out. At the door she paused and turned once more. "You know, I came in here to apologize to you."

"I highly doubt that."

"It's true." She laughed bitterly. "I actually came in here to tell you I was wrong. But, never mind."

Before Brandi got down the hall, Ash called, "You? Admitting you were wrong? I've got to hear this."

"Why should I when you're being such a bitch?"

Ash cringed. She hated who she was being right now. "Hey, Brandi," she called. "I'm sorry. I don't know why we have to do this all the time. We're grown women acting like poorly behaved teenagers."

Brandi stopped halfway down the hall before turning. "Some habits are hard to kick." Motioning with her head toward Ash's room she said, "Particularly when we're both still trapped in this place."

Did Brandi feel trapped, too? This was news to Ashley.

"All I wanted to say…" Brandi said, sighing with resignation, "was that I was wrong about you and Colton." She waved toward the computer. "Obviously."

"Yeah?"

"Yeah. So, I'm sorry for being so…"

"So mean-girlish?"

Brandi shrugged. "Whatever you want to call it." She scuffed her boot along the floor. "I was just really surprised. That's all."

"Why? Why does everyone find it so surprising that Colton and I hooked up?"

Wryly, Brandi said, "I know way too many guys like Colton Cross. A bunch of players, all of them. They don't settle down, their lifestyle won't let them, plus they don't want to."

"Yeah, well…"

"A different woman in every town." She paused to study Ashley. "Kids by different mommas in every other state."

"Brandi."

"I'm serious."

Ash shrugged. "Well, it's not like that, anyway. We're just messing around. For now."

"Okay." Brandi backed out of the doorway. "I just never pictured you with someone like him. So…be careful."

"Be careful of what?"

"Getting too attached. It doesn't matter how cool you think you can play it, once you have sex with a guy like that, it's hard not to fall in love a little."

Ashley watched her sister go down the hallway to her own bedroom. Her skin felt tight. Her stomach was making weird little rumbly noises and her throat felt itchy. Either she was coming down with something or it was already too late.

She was already way too attached to Colton.

"I am in trouble," she whispered to herself.

IT WAS A beautiful day for a wedding, not that Colton liked weddings all that much. They always landed on the weekend when he'd rather be doing a million other things, and there was too much sitting around for his liking, too many public displays of affection. But the parties were usually pretty good.

This one was looking like it was going to be less exciting. It was a small gathering. Sage and Andy, Gloria's dad, were in their sixties, not really the party types. Gloria was about to pop at any moment, so she and Dillon would be heading to bed early, and Colton and Dillon's cousin Jamie—who was supposed to attend with his wife, Daisy, who was Gloria's best friend—had had to cancel at the last minute. Like Gloria, Daisy was pregnant and the doctor had advised against travel because of high blood pressure.

Hence a snoozer of a party.

The upside of a quiet party was that he would be able to secrete away the lovely Miss Ozark and have his wicked way with her.

Seriously, he could not get enough of her.

Though he'd barely seen her today—she'd arrived early to help with the flowers, then she'd been tied up taking pictures, leaving no time for him. Didn't matter, he had the rest of the evening all planned out. He'd untie those delicate strings that were holding up the top of her dress and kiss his way down her sweet little body. How the woman could ever imagine herself to be invisible was beyond him. It didn't matter how inconspicuous she tried to be while behind the camera. She stood out and not just because she was pretty. It was like she had a light shining through every pore of her skin. She lit up the room with her presence.

She lit him up even more.

Even when he couldn't see Ashley, he could sense her: by her scent, by the way the back of his skull prickled when she stood near him.

Did she experience the same thing for him? Maybe, because while he was trying to quietly approach her from behind as she took pictures of the head table eating dinner, she stopped, dropped the camera and turned around while he was still a few steps away.

"What are you doing, skulking about?"

"I do not skulk," he said, putting on an offended tone of voice.

She smiled, but it wasn't the secret sexy one he was hoping for.

"You really need to check your texts," he said. "Because there are some good ones in there."

She held up the camera. "I'm working, if you hadn't noticed."

"Oh. I've noticed." He waved toward the subjects of her photographs. "Keep going. No reason I can't stand here while you work."

She twisted her lips in disbelief but went back to what she was doing. Angling the camera, adjusting the lens, taking pictures.

"Do you want me to tell you what I wrote in my texts?" he whispered from right behind her.

"No."

Ignoring her, he continued, "There was one…it was quite detailed, but I'll summarize. I use my teeth to undo those little straps of yours." He slipped a finger beneath the spaghetti strap and caressed her shoulder. "Then I lick every inch of you—"

"Colton," she whispered over her shoulder. "Not while I'm working." There was nothing playful about her voice now.

"You are allowed to take a break, you know. You need to eat, Ashley."

"I will eat. I just…" She looked at him over her shoulder again. Her face was pinched, like talking to him was pretty much the same thing as sucking a lemon. "You're distracting me."

"Wow." He backed off, her tone taking him by surprise. "Okay. I'll leave you alone, then."

She blinked and then looked down at the screen of her camera, fiddling with something. "I'd appreciate it." She glanced up and forced a smile. "I'll talk to you later, okay?"

"Sure thing."

Colton made his way back to the table where he was sitting with his brother, Dillon, and a few other guests. Gloria was the matron of honor so was up at the head table.

"What's wrong with you?" Dillon asked.

"Nothing." Colton sat back down and dug into the dessert that had been served while he was off talking to Ashley. At the thought of her, he glanced up, finding her immediately.

Yep. His Ashley-radar was still finely tuned, no matter how she was treating him. "I'm just getting the cold shoulder," he said with his mouth full of strawberries and cream.

"What did you do?" Dillon asked in that big-brother way that pissed Colt off.

"Not a damn thing."

"Uh-huh."

"I didn't." Colton finished the strawberry cheesecake in two bites, though he barely tasted it.

"Sometimes it's the things you *don't* do that piss a woman off more than the things you do do."

"What the hell does that mean?"

"It means that if you care about this girl, you better find out what it is that you didn't do."

16

ASHLEY TRIED TO focus on Sage and Andy, the happy couple, but all she could see were fuzzy outlines, no matter how much she adjusted the focus. And all she could hear was Colton's deep voice whispering in her ear. Suggesting deliciously naughty things.

Except Colton's sinful suggestions were interrupted by Brandi's warning, reminding her of exactly the kind of guy that Colton was.

A different woman in every town. Kids by different mommas in every other state...

Colton was a player who was using her for sex. While she'd tried to tell herself she didn't care and that she'd been using him, too, it was a lie.

The idea of saying goodbye was... Well...it was a hunk of lead growing in the pit of her stomach, weighing heavily on her and poisoning her bloodstream in the process. The fact she had a secret file of Colton pics that she obsessed over when she wasn't with him—let's face it—it was a bad sign.

And then today...

She'd blown up the picture of Gloria and Dillon and had it printed on canvas twice. One copy for Gloria and Dillon, the other as a wedding gift to Sage and Andy because it was their grandchild in Gloria's belly. She'd cried while she'd wrapped them.

Why the hell had she cried? She was not an emotional woman. Oh, she felt emotions as much as the next person, but growing up, she'd learned to hide them because the alternative was to be teased by her older sisters. Now, here she was at this wedding, chronicling the event—the late-in-life love affair—and she felt...

Cheated.

The love between Sage and Andy was so palpable she didn't even have to work to get it to show up in the photos. Soft smiles that reached right up into the eyes. Lingering touches, the need to always be in contact with one another. Laughter, the ease of being with the person you want to spend the rest of your life with. It was all a little hard to swallow.

Ash wanted that.

She deserved it.

Sure, she might be having hot, casual sex with Colton, but that was all it was ever going to be.

Ashley wanted more.

She glanced over to where Colton was sitting with Dillon, the two brothers so much alike in so many ways. Yet, like all siblings, so different. Dillon was a solid family man and Colt was...

He glanced up and caught her watching him, making it impossible to finish her thought. Ash felt the pull from across the distance. It was a visceral, powerful thing. Something she'd never felt before and something she'd certainly never expected to feel for Colton.

It took two tries to swallow past the lump in her throat, but when she finally managed, she'd made up her mind about what she needed to do. Friends with benefits was fine as long as all you really wanted was friendship.

Unfortunately, Ashley now realized she wanted more from Colton. Much more. And it would be a cold day in hell before Colton ever wanted the same from her.

"LET'S DANCE."

Colton's voice sent instant shock waves through Ashley's body. Normally those shock waves were welcome. Tonight they weren't. She'd been a fool to think she could do this with him, because the more time she spent with him, the harder it would be to leave. Worse would be Colton leaving in a couple of weeks and Ashley having to spend the rest of the summer here.

Alone.

Slowly, Ash lowered the camera from in front of her face and turned. Colton stood there with an unreadable expression on his handsome face. His hand waited, palm up, for her to take.

"Let me put my camera away first."

He waved her toward the table and then waited where he was for her to return. Though it was a warm night, Ash shivered when Colton took her hand, resting his other on her lower back.

"What did I do?" he asked after five seconds of moving around the dance floor.

"Excuse me?"

"You're acting weird. What did I do?"

Ash wet her lips, unable to meet Colton's gaze. "Nothing. You didn't do anything."

Colton mumbled something beneath his breath about being right and Dillon not knowing shit, but Ash wasn't paying too much attention because her mind was working at a million miles an hour, trying on phrases, rejecting them and trying out new ones.

I changed my mind about this whole friends-with-benefits thing...

"It looks like your job's all done for the evening." Colton pulled her close and spun her. "I suggest you take a much-needed break."

Gazing up at him, Ash thought, *I think it would be better for both of us if we just called it off. Right now...*

But Colton's hand was roving up and down her back, and it felt so damn good. She was weak when she was in Colton's arms, weaker still when she was in Colton's bed. The truth was, she'd never been so weak before in her life. Hadn't Jasmine told her about how much she looked up to her for knowing what she wanted and going after it?

Yet here she was, willing to take a night of passion over her own sanity.

"You're tense. Lucky for you I happen to know a great massage therapist."

She took a deep breath, ignoring the large, muscular hand on her back, ready to say, *Remember when I said one of us would get hurt if we took this too far? Well, one of us has...* But the breath she'd inhaled exited without any words attached.

"He's very good at full-body massages," Colton whispered. "Extremely thorough." His hand dropped to her ass.

Oh, God. It was too much. "Stop." Her voice was sharp and—dammit—emotional.

The immediate effect of her tone was that Colton stopped moving, causing a couple to bump into them on the dance floor.

"What's going on, Ash?"

She searched the tent frantically. She couldn't do this here.

"We need to talk."

Taking Colt's hand, she pulled him toward the tent exit, past where the fairy lights lit up the trees to a bench down by the pond.

C'mon Ash, you can do it.

She gazed up at him and placed her hand on his chest, which was a mistake because he looked so damn handsome in his suit, and his chest was so wonderfully strong and broad...

"I've got a job offer in Des Moines. I leave in two days." Oh. My. God. Where had that come from?

"That's kind of sudden, isn't it?"

She shrugged. "It just came up."

"When?"

"Umm...yesterday."

"And you waited until right now to tell me?"

Yeah, she waited until now because it had just popped into her head. Here she was, lying her face off again. That's what Colton did to her. Made her into someone she wasn't. Someone who had to lie. Even now, when she should be fessing up, she couldn't.

"I didn't think it'd matter. You're leaving in a week and a half yourself. We knew this was coming. Does it really make a difference who leaves first?"

Colton's brows drew together. He stood and held out his hand for her to take. Without thinking, she reached for him.

"If that's the way it's got to be, we'd better go." He pulled her toward the barn.

Ash dug in her high heels. "Where are we going?"

"Where do you think? I'm taking you back to my bunk-house so we can say goodbye properly."

She yanked her hand from his and shook her head, an overwhelming need to be with Colton warring with an equally overwhelming need to get as far away from him as possible. "No."

"No?"

"I can't, Colton."

"Why not?"

Because if I sleep with you one more time, I won't be able to say goodbye, and then when you leave I'll be crushed.

What she said was, "We're going to say goodbye now."

"Don't make me pick you up again," he said, making a grab for her.

She gave him a shove, angry now. Sometimes his bossy, selfish attitude turned her on; right now all it was doing was pushing her buttons and making her desperate. "I said, no."

"Ash?"

"Look, I have an early morning last shift at the flower shop…" Oh, God. She'd have to let Leslie know she was leaving. "I need to pack and…" Ash mentally added the money from the wedding contract to her savings and her last pay check from the flower shop. It wasn't as much as she'd wanted saved, but she could make it work. "I've got so much to do."

Such an understatement.

Colt reached for her hand, but she tugged it away. Turning so he wouldn't see her face, she made her way back to the reception tent where her camera bag had been left.

"Ashley," he called. "For fuck's sake. At least say goodbye to me."

"Goodbye, Colton," she called over her shoulder, praying he wouldn't catch up to her again and see the tears running down her cheeks.

Colton sat in Dillon's office, surfing the internet. Okay, maybe not surfing because he knew exactly what he was looking for: *America's Best Kept Secrets—A Photo Blog*.

Sure enough, she'd gone to Des Moines. There was no mention on her blog about what job she'd been contracted for, but already, she'd found a bunch of places—gems he'd never heard of—en route to Des Moines. A nature park in South Dakota that looked like some mystical place out of a fairy tale, a suspension bridge and some really cool caves in Iowa, among others. Every place she showcased was a place he now wanted to see because they looked so damned appealing in her photographs. Mind you, Ashley was so talented she could make any run-of-the-mill place look amazing. It was all in the lighting, the angle, the... he couldn't even put his finger on it.

Colt clicked on the About section—like he'd done a few hundred times a day since she'd left—and touched the image of her that popped up. It was one of the photos he'd taken when he'd wrestled the camera out of her hands up at the Doghouse. Considering how talented she was, the picture of her was amateurish—his fault—but he loved it.

It was bizarre how when he'd first seen her again and hadn't recognized her, he'd thought she was kind of plain, nondescript. Ordinary.

Now when he looked at her picture all he saw was the sexy, hardworking, playful and passionate woman he'd come to know. Intimately. In the picture she was smiling that sexy smile that was just for him. The one that hinted at secrets—dirty secrets—and was in wonderful contrast to her overall appearance of innocence.

"You are anything but innocent," he muttered to the screen.

"Text her."

Colton jumped.

Dillon must have taken off his boots because normally his older brother sounded like a herd of elephants walking across the hard wood. There was no point covering up the fact he was stalking Ashley, so he left the website up and clicked on the images she'd taken of the Iowa State Rodeo.

"She's really good," Dillon commented.

"Yep."

"So...stop moping and text her."

"Why?" Colton stood. "What's the point?"

"The point is, you really like this girl. Make an effort for once."

"An effort? I leave for Wyoming in two days."

"The qualifier?"

"Yep."

"You know, the tour isn't all it's cracked up to be." Dillon arched his back painfully.

"That's fine for you to say. You got your chance to live your dream. I want mine." He pointed at the computer. "And Ashley wants hers, too. Unfortunately, our dreams don't—" he crisscrossed his fingers and then pulled them apart "—collide."

Dillon sighed and clapped him on the back. "You do what you have to do, Colt. But my advice is if you want to get over her? Stop stalking her."

It was good advice. Probably. The crazy thing was, they'd only hung out for a few weeks. Certainly not enough time to develop any real feelings.

"C'mon. I've got some gear I've been meaning to give you for the road."

Colton followed Dillon out of the office, through the great room. A large canvas print hanging over the fireplace caught his eye because it was new.

He stopped to look, and it was like the image kicked him in the gut.

It was a photo of Gloria and Dillon with Dillon kneeling before his pregnant wife and the sun shining in the window haloing her like some ethereal creature. The reaction to the image was instant and visceral, and Colton figured it had nothing to do with his brother and sister-in-law, and everything to do with the photographer. In his mind's eye, he saw her so clearly. The woman behind the camera. Quietly capturing magic.

The most amazing woman he'd ever met and could never have.

Ash looked at her map, tracing the options with her finger. East into Illinois? North into Minnesota? South into

Missouri? This was not exactly the route she'd originally intended to take, straight into the heart of the Midwest, but when you told lies off the top of your head, you kind of had to roll with it.

It had taken her a week to drive to Iowa, making unlikely stops at lesser known attractions in South Dakota, and she'd spent another week in Iowa, taking a couple of days in Des Moines to check out their local rodeo and fair and see how it compared to Half Moon.

So far the trip was everything she had hoped for. She'd met some really nice people, had seen some cool things, had unfortunately spent more than she'd intended on food and accommodations, which would have to change.

However, even after two weeks away there was still a molten ball of lead in her stomach.

I'll get over him eventually.

She opened her contacts and typed in Colton's name.

His info came up with his last name displayed as Best Boyfriend Ever.

Her finger hovered over the delete contact key when her phone beeped, alerting her to a new message.

She canceled what she was about to do and checked the new message, her heart in her throat as it had been every time her message app beeped.

Not from Colton. Jasmine.

Call me.

Ash stared at the message for a moment, and before she could make up her mind about what to do, her phone rang. It was Jasmine.

"Hey, Jazz," she said.

"When were you going to tell me you were in the area?" Jasmine asked before even greeting her.

"How'd you know?"

"I follow your blog. Duh."

"Oh. Well, I was going to let you know, but this job came up out of the blue."

"What job?"

Oh, seriously. The lies. She had to stop this. Yet did she? No. "It was for the Des Moines Rodeo and Fair." Ashley pinched the bridge of her nose. God.

"So? When will you be in Chicago? It's only five hours away, and you can stay with me. Parker's in Australia for two weeks."

Ash tapped her pencil against the map, reminded of how Jasmine's fiancé hadn't invited her to London and how hurt she'd been.

"You can help me pick out a wedding dress. Please, Ash."

"Okay. I'll be there in a few days."

She smiled at the delighted sound of Jasmine's squeal on the other end of the line.

"Planning a wedding is just so much more fun with your best friend."

"I'm happy to help."

"And I would be happy to return the favor...one day."

Ash covered her face. The hot thing in the pit of her belly liquefied, making everything sour. "Sure thing, Jazz. I'll see you in a few days."

17

COLTON STOOD ON the stoop of the old warehouse in a run-down area of Chicago and rang the doorbell. Someone he didn't know opened the door.

"Can I help you?"

"Yeah. I'm supposed to meet my cousins here. Jamie and Colin Forsythe."

The guy looked him over. "You Dillon's little brother?"

Considering he was as tall, if not taller, than Dillon, he took offense at being referred to as little. "I'm his *brother*, Colton," he said solemnly.

The guy didn't pay any attention to his tone. He simply greeted him and opened the door wide for him to enter. "I think Jamie's over by the ring, waiting to spar."

"Thanks." Colton made his way to the center of the room where the boxing ring was. He'd only been to his cousin's private boxing club once before, but as soon as he'd qualified for the tour in Wyoming and had subsequently qualified for the Chicago Invitational, he knew this was the first place he had to visit.

His cousin Jamie was standing ringside, watching the bout between his twin brother, Colin, and a man Colton didn't know. It took Colton jabbing Jamie on the arm for his cousin to notice him.

"Colt?" His face split into a grin, and he gave him a back-patting, manly hug. "How you doing?"

"Great. I'm good."

"I hear you've made it pro. Congratulations."

Colton nodded, his eyes straying to the bout in the ring while he shifted from foot to foot. "Thanks. It's been a long time coming."

Using his chin to indicate the ring, Jamie asked, "You here just to visit or you planning on changing and going a round or two in the ring?"

Rubbing his knuckles Colt replied, "Oh, I'm going to spar. Ever since I found out I made the tour, I've got all this crazy energy that needs a good outlet."

"That's why we built this." He pointed to the back of the warehouse. "You remember where the change rooms are?"

"Yep."

"You want to go a couple rounds with me?"

"If you don't mind having your ass kicked, I'd love that."

"Go get changed, little cousin, and we'll see about whose ass is going to get kicked."

With his gym bag slung over his shoulder, he ambled through the gym, past the heavy bags, the speed bags, the weight benches and stretching mats to the change room. He promptly changed into a T-shirt and shorts, thinking about the lie he'd told Jamie.

The crazy, pent-up energy he was feeling had nothing to do with making the tour and everything to do with the fact that he was in Chicago and so was Ashley. He knew because he was still stalking her. Well, it wasn't stalking if you followed her blog like a legitimate person…except that he'd created a fake email address in order to sign up for her updates.

It was weird. He'd told Dillon their paths wouldn't cross, and yet here they were, both in Chicago at the same time. There were rolls of tape stacked in a shelf, and Colton helped himself to some and began taping up his hands.

He could feel her presence, just like he'd always been

able to. Every street corner he looked over his shoulder, expecting to see her because he had the prickly feeling on the back of his neck. He finished winding tape around his left hand and bit it to tear it off. Then he started on his right.

Why did it make him think of winding tape around Ashley's wrists and securing them to a bedpost? Of licking his way down her body and driving her so frickin' crazy her little body bucked like a young bronc while she screamed his name?

He groaned. Goddamn it, he should not be thinking such thoughts before a fight. He should be focusing on expelling some of this angst and concentrating on competing in two days' time.

Thinking about taping up the sexiest, wildest, most passionate woman he'd ever met was not conducive to relieving angst.

Text her.

Dillon's voice was in his head, taunting him.

"Okay," he muttered before biting off the last bit of tape. "I'll text her, but not until after my ride. I can't have her distracting me like she did last time."

"Oh, I LIKE that one," Ashley said as Jasmine twisted back and forth in front of the mirror on the little stage the bridal shop had set up. "It's very pretty."

"You've said that about the last ten."

Seeing her reflection, Ash read the guilty expression on her features. "Sorry, Jazz. They're all starting to look the same."

"I know, right?" Jazz made a face as she twisted once more. Turning to the woman who'd been helping them, she shook her head. "I think we're done for the day."

Ash waited on the couch drinking tea while Jazz changed back into her street clothes. Once her friend emerged from the dressing room, Ash said, "It wasn't a lie, you know. You look amazing in all of those dresses. I don't know how you'll choose."

Jazz shrugged. "Yeah. I don't either. Nothing's really stood out for me."

Ash observed her friend closely. On the tip of her tongue was the question she'd been dying to ask Jasmine. Was she having second thoughts? Did she still think of Curtis? Did she really want to get married in the first place?

But she didn't. It wasn't the kind of conversation you wanted to have in the parking lot of a bridal boutique.

They were quiet on the drive back to Jasmine's luxury apartment until after they'd parked and taken the elevator up to the sixteenth floor. Maybe that's what thousands of wedding dresses did to a person. Made them incapable of forming sentences.

Jasmine's apartment was located in Dearborn Park, a trendy part of Chicago. With an incredible view of Lake Michigan, the place had to have cost a fortune. Ash hazarded a glance at her friend who was discussing takeout places for dinner that night.

"I'm easy," Ash said. "You know best."

"Indian food okay with you? There's a little place I found that's almost as good as my Auntie Rehana's cooking."

"Sounds wonderful."

Just as Jasmine was putting in an order, Ashley's phone rang.

Her stomach lurched—as it did with every unexpected text or phone call. "Hello?" Her voice was breathy.

"Ashley Ozark?"

"Yes?"

"This is Linda Tomlin from the NBRA publicity department."

"How can I help you?"

"We were given your contact information from Buck Stevens. He's a board member for the NBRA—"

"NBRA?"

"National Bull Riding Association. Anyway, he was a guest judge at the Beaverhead County Rodeo and raved about the work you did there as photographer. We need a freelancer for the Chicago Invitational on Saturday. Are you interested?"

Ashley nearly dropped her phone in surprise. It slid down her face, and she caught it before it landed on the floor.

"Are you serious?"

"Yes. One of our regulars just broke his leg. I know it's short notice but—"

"I'll do it."

"Don't you want to hear the terms first?"

"Right. Yes." Ashley listened to the offer. It didn't pay a whole hell of a lot, and she could probably have negotiated for more, but she didn't care. It was a huge opportunity.

Once she was off the phone, she realized that Jasmine was watching her with a strange expression on her face. "Congratulations." She forced a smile. "Things are really happening for you."

"Yeah. I can't believe it…" Ash tamped down her excitement and said, "What's going on, Jazz?"

"What do you mean?"

"You are not yourself."

"Of course I am."

"No. You're not. The Jasmine I love would know exactly what kind of dress she wanted. She would be loving every second of trying on millions of dresses. She would know her colors, her flowers…" She grabbed Jasmine's hand. "You don't have to get married if you don't want to."

"I know."

"So? Do you even want to marry Parker?" Ash had

almost said, "the elusive Parker," because as far as she could tell, the man was never around.

"Of course. He's perfect. I mean, we have this totally perfect life."

"Except…"

Jasmine blinked. Then, making her way toward the refrigerator, she said, "Sex is bad," in a completely monotone voice as if she wasn't confessing something huge. She opened the fridge and took out a bottle of Perrier and poured two glasses.

Ash followed, opening the fridge door just after it closed and pulling out a chilled bottle of wine. "I think this conversation requires alcohol."

"You might be right." Jazz filled two enormous glasses almost to the top. Taking a seat on the stool at the counter, she took a long drink of wine.

"How bad is bad?" Ash asked, watching Jazz guzzle the wine like it was grape juice.

"Pretty bad." She drew a circle across the countertop with her manicured nail. "We barely do it, and when we do?" She raised her eyes and made a face. "Bleh."

"Surely it can't be that bad."

Jasmine's face lost all its sparkle. "It is."

"Is that why you kissed Curtis?"

"Probably." She paused. "I needed to know if it was me."

"Oh, Jazz. It's not you." Ash leaned over and hugged her friend as Jasmine made sad snuffling sounds against her shoulder.

"You know, I might not have even realized how bad things were until I saw you and Colton." Jazz moved back, wiping tears off her cheek, leaving dark mascara streaks in her wake.

A lump formed in Ashley's throat at the mention of

Colton's name. "What do you mean?" she asked, her own voice quivering.

"He's always touching you. Kissing you." Her perfect nose wrinkled. "Even sniffing you, for God's sake."

"Oh, Jazz—" Ash said, putting her hand on Jasmine's arm. "Please, don't compare Colton to—"

"It's the way he looks at you." Jasmine just carried right on. "Like he wants to eat you up."

Ash groaned inwardly.

"When you weren't looking, he'd watch you, like he was imagining all the things he'd do to you later…"

"Stop."

"Parker never looks at me like that."

"Jazz…about Colton…"

"It's so obvious he loves you. With Parker—"

"Jazz." Ashley had to raise her voice to get her friend to stop talking.

"What?"

Ash took a deep drink of wine. And then another. She set her glass down and stared into the clear liquid. "Colton doesn't love me." With a sigh, she met Jasmine's gaze. "Colton's not even my boyfriend."

"Oh, no. The two of you broke up? That's terrible."

Ash shook her head. "Hard to break up when we weren't even going out."

"What are you talking about?"

Shutting her eyes for a second to bolster her courage, Ash blurted out. "It was all a lie."

"What was a lie?"

"Colton. He was fake. We weren't dating. I coerced him into playing my boyfriend." She paused to rub her forehead. "No, it's worse than that. I *paid* him to be my boyfriend."

"What?"

"Stupid, right?"

"But…why would you do that?"

"To impress you."

"Me?"

"Yes." Ash shook her head. "You have this amazing life." She gestured toward the room at large. "You always have. And I have…nothing."

Jasmine stared at her for a moment and then started laughing. There was a touch of hysteria to it. "We are quite a pair, aren't we?"

"Yeah." Ash tried to laugh along, but it was halfhearted.

"Well, let me tell you something. Maybe you and Colton didn't start out having feelings for each other, but looks and actions don't lie." Jasmine covered Ash's hand with hers. "That man loves you, Ashley, and you'd be a fool to let that kind of love go so easily." She patted. "Text him."

ASH DIDN'T TEXT Colton. She couldn't. What would be the point? He had his stuff going on and she had hers. She wasn't about to drop everything she'd worked so hard for, for a guy she wasn't even sure liked her or had the ability to commit to any kind of relationship whatsoever.

I'm no good at commitment or relationships, Ash…

Though being at the Chicago Invitational Bull Riding Event made *not* thinking about him impossible. Particularly when she saw his name on the contestant roster. So he'd qualified for the pro tour; good for him.

Her stomach twisted as she glanced around the crowded arena, hoping for a glimpse of his familiar stance, his familiar gait. The breadth of his shoulders. God, she could feel him. Practically smell his spicy aftershave.

She took a look at her contact list, tapping in Colton's name.

Best Boyfriend Ever.

God. So tempting. Just a quick little "Hello! You'll never guess where I am!"

A horn sounded, and Ash reminded herself that she had a job to do. Her job was to take pictures and then immediately post them to Twitter and Instagram. She was the event's social media photo specialist. Just for the day.

Ash connected the camera to the tablet she'd been given and found the best ones of Olsen Hammer, who'd just ridden, and posted with the commentary, "Things are getting wild at the Chicago Invitational."

Once done, she stuck the tablet back in her bag and wiped her hands down the front of her jeans. There were only two more contestants until Colton. The first, a cowboy from Kentucky, got thrown right out of the gate. The second hung on for the entire eight seconds.

It was Colton's turn, and her heart was in her throat. Using the telephoto lens, Ash brought him into focus. God, she could see every line on his face, the groove between his brows as he climbed atop the bull in the chute. She had no idea how many pictures she took; her finger depressed the shutter all on its own while she watched him, like she was right there. His focused expression. His determination. The simple nod to show he was ready.

Her heart pounded between her ears as she waited for the gate to open.

The second the door swung wide, the bull shot out like the chute was a cannon: running a few steps before its hind end moved as if quite separate from the rest of it. Was she even taking pictures? She couldn't tell as she followed the sporadic movements around the ring from behind her camera.

Eight seconds seemed impossibly long.

Finally the buzzer rang, and Colt dove for one of the horses that rode out to flank the bull, easily landing on his feet as the other cowboy corralled the livestock out of the ring.

Click.

Ash checked the final image, Colton standing near the gates, his hat in hand waving to the huge crowd. To her, it looked as if he was staring right at her. Like he could see her amidst the throng of people. Like his cocky grin was just for her.

Without realizing what she was doing, she kissed the image of him on the little screen, making the camera slip from her fingers. Thank God she wore the neck strap; otherwise her most valuable piece of equipment would have shattered on the cement floor. That would have been a tragedy.

Wiping her palms once more, she lifted the camera to her face and looked through the lens again, trying to locate Colton as he left the arena.

"Best Boyfriend Ever?" she said with a chuckle as she caught sight of him climbing the bleacher stairs behind the chutes. She zoomed in even closer. "Doubtful. But the nicest ass in town? Oh, yeah. Definitely."

18

COLTON WAS WALKING on air. His feet didn't even touch the ground as he made his way up the stairs to the bleachers after his ride.

His very first pro ride and he'd nailed it. Now he just had to wait to see how his score compared.

Somehow, his dream had come true. Finally.

"Colton, up here!" He glanced up. A few rows over was a pretty, dark-haired woman.

"Daisy?"

The woman excused herself to the others in the row as she made her way toward him. No easy feat when she was pregnant and well past her due date. She was breathing heavily when she greeted him in the aisle.

"Hey, little cousin! That was an amazing ride. I'm so proud of you!"

Colton grabbed Daisy and lifted her up. It wasn't something he'd planned to do; it was just something he needed to do to expend some of this adrenaline and excitement.

"Where's Jamie, that ugly husband of yours?" he asked after setting Daisy down.

"He's getting me ice cream and a hot dog. Oh, and popcorn." Daisy tapped her lips. "And donuts." She smoothed her hands over her basketball-sized belly. "His son is hungry." She made a face. "Oh. And he's restless." She rubbed some more as a beatific look came over her features. "Want to feel?"

"Sure, why not?" He let Daisy guide his hands over her stomach where he felt the strangest sensation of movement beneath his hands. "Oh, my God."

"It's crazy, right? It's like I've got an alien in me."

"When is the alien landing on Earth?"

"Supposed to be last week." She winked. "Things must be a little too cozy up in there."

Colton was happy for Daisy. In fact, Colton was happy, period. Life was good. He was on the pro tour now, his cousins were happily married and about to have a baby. His brother and sister-in-law were the same. When things were this good it was important to take a moment to appreciate it, which he did by leaning down to kiss Daisy on the cheek.

And then things just got better.

"Ashley Ozark to the announcer's booth on the mezzanine level. Ashley Ozark to the announcer's booth."

Colton couldn't believe his luck. It was like the universe had orchestrated all of this: the ride, her presence, this town, this place. It was all meant to be, and now it felt like the universe was telling him through the damn loudspeaker that it was no coincidence that Ashley—the woman he could not stop stalking online—just happened to be here on what might very well be the best day of his life.

"Hey, Daisy, I'll catch up with you and Jamie later, okay?"

"Where you going?"

"I have to go see about a woman."

"Oh? Anyone special?"

"Yeah." Colton patted his hand over his heart, mimicking a heartbeat. "Very special."

She waved him off. "What the hell are you waiting for, then? Get going."

ASHLEY WALKED LIKE a zombie to the announcer's booth: dragging her feet and making soft moaning sounds with every step as she made her way up to the mezzanine level. Once there, the man told her to wait, and he disappeared inside. Ashley leaned against the wall feeling…numb.

Maybe she'd made a mistake. Maybe it wasn't him.

Attaching the cord of her camera to the tablet, she downloaded the latest pictures and then enlarged the last two.

It was him all right. One with him lifting up a woman— much like he'd once lifted her—before kissing her. Another photo with his hands on the woman's belly, practically a carbon copy of the photo she'd taken of his brother and sister-in-law where the joy between the two was palpable.

A different woman in every town. Kids by different mommas in every other state.

Why did Brandi have to be right about Colton?

Ashley's phone pinged. She closed the images on the tablet and checked her messages.

Oh, God. No.

The message was from *Colton Best Boyfriend Ever.*

"Asshole."

She opened it.

I heard your name announced. You're here? We have to meet up. There's something I need to tell you.

"What? You want to introduce me to your girlfriend and child?" She pinched the bridge of her nose.

Ash supposed that was exactly how guys like Colton operated, not thinking twice about the fact that if you slept with a woman, she was going to become emotionally attached. He didn't care how she felt, which was how he managed to live the way he did.

She was an idiot.

The door to the announcer's room opened, and Linda Tomlin, the head of publicity, appeared. "Ashley, great to see you."

"Is everything okay?" Ash asked. The only reason she could think that they would be calling her up here in the middle of the job was to fire her.

Which pretty much made this the worst day of her life.

"Everything is amazing. We've just learned that your Tweets and posts are getting way more hits and interaction than we've ever had."

"Really?"

Linda smiled. "Yeah, really. So, we want to offer you a six-month contract to keep doing what you're doing. If you do well, we'll talk about extending it even more."

Ash gave her head a shake. A contract? To work for the NBRA? To get paid to do the thing she loved most?

It was a dream come true, which was probably why she gasped in utter shock.

"Shall I take that as a yes?" Linda chuckled.

Ash glanced around, feeling ecstatic and...trapped.

Accepting the contract would mean she'd be on the tour with Colton. What if he tried to seduce her again? Would she be strong enough to resist?

Hell, no.

Even now she wanted him. Desperately. But then what? It wasn't like he'd want her around full-time.

I'm no good at commitment or relationships, Ash. I've never understood it.

The worse thing Ash could imagine was having to witness what she'd seen here tonight in town after town. Colton talking to other women. Colton flirting with other woman. Colton becoming a daddy, for fuck's sake.

"So," Linda prompted. "What do you think?"

Ash blinked away the flashing images of Colton inside

her head. "It all sounds amazing." She met Linda's gaze. "But I can't do it. I'm sorry."

COLTON DIDN'T GET IT. He was dressed in his gym clothes and had made another visit to his cousins' private gym. Working on the heavy bag, he completed a jab, jab, cross combo.

What the hell happened?

Pretending the bag was an opponent, he turned on autopilot, pummeling the thing while in his mind, he reviewed the series of texts that had been sent between himself and Ashley last night.

I heard your name announced. You're here? We have to meet up. There's something I need to tell you.

He'd waited half an hour for her to reply. When she didn't he sent another one.

Ash? I know you're here. Let's meet up.

Nothing.
He'd tried calling but the call went to voice mail.

Ash? I really have to see you.
Ash, I need you.

Finally, a reply came in. Stop texting, Colton, and go live your life.

It made no sense. Unless...

Was it possible that Ashley had no feelings for him? When she'd said goodbye, did she really mean it? He let go of a flurry of punches, knocking the bag off-kilter so that it swung at him sideways. Wrapping his arms around it, Colton hugged it to get it to stop swinging.

"You know that bag doesn't hit back," Colin, his other cousin, said. "You feel like sparring?"

"Only if you feel like getting the shit kicked out of you."

Colin laughed. "You're in a fine mood." He gestured toward the now-empty ring. "I'm pretty sure a good fight is exactly what you need."

Colt climbed into the ring after his cousin. They went to face each other in the middle, bumping gloves first before dancing away from one another. Colin threw a couple of tentative jabs, just to test Colton's reflexes and his blocking.

"You going to tell me what's wrong?" Colin asked.

"Nothing." Colt jabbed twice lightly with his left before releasing his right uppercut.

Colin blocked it easily, sliding away before Colton could get him up against the ropes. "Is it a woman?"

When Colton answered with a flurry of crosses, most of which landed on Colin's arms, not Colt's intended targets, Colin chuckled. His mouth guard fell out of his mouth on to the floor of the ring.

"What is wrong with women?" Colt asked as he waited for Colin to wash the plastic mouth guard off with a spray from a water bottle.

"Not sure there's a general ailment for *all* women." Colin smirked over his shoulder. "What's the deal with this *particular* one?"

"She won't respond to my messages."

Colin groaned. "Do you know what the all-time *worst* invention for relationships is?"

Colt shook his head.

"Text messaging." Colin squirted a shot of water into his mouth. "My advice? Go see this woman. In person. Talk to her, the old-fashioned way." He settled his guard back into his mouth so his next sentence came out sounding garbled. "In the meantime, focus on the fight, because if you don't, I'm going to kick your scrawny ass all the way back to Half Moon Creek."

AFTER A TEARFUL farewell with Jasmine, Ashley made the drive home to Half Moon Creek. The thing about driving for hours and hours on end, listening to a playlist she'd created—every sad and angry song in her library—meant Ashley not only knew all the words to all the songs by the end of the twenty-one hours, she'd also had plenty of time to think.

She'd been mad. Fuming. Her foot heavy on the gas pedal as she sang along to Carrie Underwood's "Before He Cheats." But somewhere between Bismarck, North Dakota, and Miles City, Montana, Ashley realized something important.

Colton didn't owe her anything.

He had always been her *pretend* boyfriend and nothing more. Well, there was the very short friends-with-benefits stage. But she had to put the emphasis on *friends*. That was it. That was all they'd ever had.

It's because he's the first guy to ever make you fall apart, a voice that sounded suspiciously like her sister's whispered in her head.

"That's a lie," Ash said aloud. "It was more than that." At least for her it was.

On the other hand, Colton had never once said he wanted more from her. He'd never claimed that he didn't see other women. He'd never committed anything to her.

Maybe if you'd told him how you felt...

Would that have changed things? Ash doubted it. Except for maybe scaring him off. How could she expect Colton to be anything except the man he was? She couldn't. But neither could she be anyone else, either, and the truth of the matter was, she was in love with him.

That's why she couldn't take the job offer. That's why

she couldn't see him again. It hurt too damn much, and she felt like a fool for falling for him even when she knew the kind of man he was.

I'll send you the contract, anyway, Linda had said after being surprised by Ashley's response. *Think about it for a few days and get back to me by the end of the week.*

Ash didn't need a few days.

Between Miles City and Bozeman, Montana, Ash came up with a plan to go forward. She would stay in Half Moon for the rest of the summer, earning money like she'd originally planned, being there for Jasmine's wedding—if it even happened—and then leaving in the fall, following the original route she'd mapped out, starting on the West Coast and moving east, up and down through the states.

No more lies. No more half-truths. She would not let a man interfere with her plans again. In fact, when she got home, she was going to purge Colton Cross from her system and start over.

So, when Ash finally turned onto the street she'd grown up on, she didn't feel quite as downtrodden as she imagined she might have felt. When she carried her bags up to the porch, only to have Brandi open the door for her, she actually was thankful for her older sister's arms opening to her.

"You were right, Brandi," she whispered.

Brandi rubbed her back. "I know. And sometimes I hate the fact that I'm right all the time."

Ash didn't even know she was crying until after Brandi had said that, making her laugh through her tears. "I should have listened to you."

With a wry smile, Brandi said, "You never have before. Why start now?" She motioned toward the inside of the house. "You look exhausted. Come in and I'll make you something to eat."

19

COLTON'S EYE, THAT had been sore and swollen after the fight with Colin, now felt like it was filled with sand. He'd barely slept in the last twenty-four hours, only stopping at rest stops en route back to Montana. After the fight, he'd checked Ashley's blog and was surprised to find that she'd posted a message to followers that she'd be taking a short hiatus and returning to blog in the fall.

He made a call to Dillon and Gloria to get Jasmine's information, and it had been Jasmine who told him Ashley was on her way home.

He should probably have stopped for a shower first, but instead he found himself driving down Ashley's street, parking and walking up to her porch, ringing the bell of the Ozark residence.

His chest heaved when the door opened and then filled with disappointment when Brandi stood there instead of Ashley.

"What do you want?"

"Is Ashley home?"

"No." Brandi stuck her fists on her hips. "But even if she was, I wouldn't tell you."

Her words felt like a slap. "Why?"

"You know why, asshole."

Colton tilted his head to one side. "No, I don't."

"Don't play dumb." She squinted at him. Hard. "You

know, Ashley's not like all those other girls. You can't just use her."

"I'm not using her."

"Oh, really."

"Look. I don't know what she told you, but I didn't use her." He felt like mentioning that if anyone had been using anyone in this situation, it was Ashley when she asked him to pretend to be her boyfriend. But pointing that out would probably not be helpful right now.

"Look—" he rubbed the back of his neck "—I really need to talk to her."

"And what would you talk about, exactly?" She tilted her head to one side. "Perhaps the fact that you're going to be a daddy?" She gave him a shove. "Don't you think that's a talk you should have had long ago?"

"What?" Colton fell against the frame of the door, not from the force of Brandi's shove but from the power behind her words. He took a deep breath and regained his balance. "Where is she? Please tell me."

"*Please*? Okay, okay. Quarry Road. By the swimming hole." He released her, and she straightened her collar. With a sneer, she added, "She's purging you from her system."

"What the fuck does that mean?"

"Why don't you go find out, Daddy-O?"

Colton didn't say another word to Brandi. Didn't thank her, nothing. He turned and sprinted down the path to his truck, hopped into the driver's seat and started it, pulling away with a spray of gravel, doing a U-turn in the middle of the street so he could head out of town toward Quarry Road.

Holy mother of hell.

No wonder Ashley had acted so weird. No wonder she hated him and didn't want to talk to him. She was pregnant with his child.

Only one thing to do in this situation when a woman was carrying his baby.

He was going to have to ask that woman to marry him.

THERE WAS ALREADY a circle of rocks set up for a fire pit right on the lip of the quarry above the swimming hole. Ash gathered as much dead fall as she could find, and once she had a nice little blaze going, she pulled the stack of prints out of her backpack and went through them one by one.

Colton forking hay.

"Bye, bye, bastard," Ash said as she stuck a corner into the fire and watched the colorful flames lick across the photo paper. "Too damn hot for your own good."

The next ten were all from the rodeo, a sequence of pictures from Colton getting ready inside the chute to him being whipped around on the back of a bull.

"Adios, amigo." Ash watched each one go up in smoke.

There were forty pictures altogether. It wasn't enough to erase the images from her hard drive; she had to burn them symbolically. She had to let Colton Cross go.

For good.

She was so absorbed in what she was doing, she didn't hear the sound of the truck coming down the road. Even the crunch of footsteps on gravel went unnoticed because of the pop and sizzle of the burning photos.

"What are you doing, Ash?"

She looked up. Somehow, even though she hadn't heard his approach, Ashley was not surprised to see Colton there. Like her symbolic purging had evoked old pagan magic that made him materialize in front of her.

"Can't you tell?" She indicated the floating bits of singed photo paper. "I'm turning you into Ash." *Like me*.

Colton knelt down beside her. A concerned look on his face. "Why didn't you tell me?"

"Tell you what?"

"C'mon, Ash. You should never have kept this from me."

"Kept what?"

"When you first learned about the baby. You should have told me."

Seriously? She gave him a shove. "Why is it *my* job to bring it up with you? Don't you think that's your job?"

"Hard to bring it up when I didn't even know about it."

"Like I believe that." Ash paused because the emotions flitting across Colton's features were confusing.

Concern?

Gravity?

Responsibility?

What the hell was he doing here instead of in Chicago with the woman who looked like she was about to have a baby any second?

She went through the pictures in her hands and found the one she was looking for. She looked at it, trying to see it through new eyes. "So, you're saying you just found out about the baby at this moment?" She handed it to him. "And that was your reaction?" She pointed at the expression of joy on his face as he bent down to touch the woman's rounded stomach.

"What are you…" Colton frowned down at the picture. "Where did you get this?"

"I took it. In Chicago."

He met her gaze. Blinked. Then shook his head. "Ash… are *you* pregnant?"

"Me?" She placed her hand on her chest. "No. God, no."

He held up the picture. "And are you saying you think this woman is pregnant with my child?"

Ash wet her lips, suddenly uncertain. "Yes?"

"Do you know who this is?"

"A random woman you knocked up, I'm guessing."

Jabbing his finger into the image, Colton said, "This is my cousin's wife, Daisy. She's Gloria's best friend. She is not, nor has she ever been, my girlfriend."

"That's not your baby?"

"No. Fuck, no."

"Shit." Ashley snatched the picture from Colton's hands. "So...you didn't knock up some woman?"

"No. God."

She plopped herself down on the grass, sitting cross-legged on the lip of the swimming hole. "Okay." She blinked a couple of times, trying to make sense of everything. "So what are you doing here?"

"Honestly?" He rubbed the back of his neck, going to stand at the edge of the short cliff, looking down at the clear waters below.

Ash got up and joined him. "Yes. Honestly. You thought I was pregnant and you came up here to do what?"

He glanced down at her. "I was going to ask you to marry me."

It was like he'd clubbed her, except not in a bad way... exactly. Though breathing was impossible for a couple of seconds. "What?" she finally managed to stutter.

"Brandi said you were pregnant and I—" Tilting his head to one side, Colton considered things for a moment. "Maybe that wasn't *exactly* what she said. She just insinuated I was going to be a daddy." Colton slapped his forehead. "Oh, my God. She knew about the picture."

Ash nodded. But she couldn't quite get over what Colton had said. "So...you thought I was pregnant."

"Yes."

"And, you came up here to ask me to marry you?"

Colt rubbed his jaw "Yeah. I did."

Holy hell. Could she have been this totally wrong about Colton? Was he really as noble as he was currently pretending to be?

What if it wasn't pretend?

What if it was real?

Suddenly, a crazy idea sprang into Ashley's head. "Okay."

His brows drew together. "Okay, what?"

"Propose." She smiled so wide her cheeks hurt.

"What? But...well, ah..."

She put her hands on her hips. "C'mon. If you're going to do it, do it." She waited, tapping her toe, barely able to contain the mirth building inside of her.

With a groan, Colt dropped to one knee in front of her. He swallowed. His face was serious, and sweat had broken out on his forehead. "Um, Ashley Ozark?"

"Yes?"

"Would you...ah...do me the great honor of...ah...becoming my—"

She didn't let him finish. Instead, she pushed him over the lip of the quarry and into the swimming hole down below, where he made a thunderous splash.

He sputtered to the surface moments later. "What the hell was that?"

"That was my answer," she called. "It's no, by the way. But you're welcome to try again at a later date." Then she did a little hop and a skip and dove down into the clear water beside him.

THE SECOND COLTON opened the bunkhouse door for Ashley, she smelled something familiar. Something delicious.

"Is that...?"

"Coconut oil?" Colton grinned. "Yep. I seem to remember someone liking it."

Ash pressed her lips together to keep from smiling too wide. "And what, pray tell, do you plan to do with that coconut oil?"

"I will show you as soon as you take off your clothes."

Colton came forward and starting undoing the buttons on her top.

"Sounds like a trap." She teased, halfheartedly slapping his hands away.

"No trap. It's more like a reward. Which I will give you once you give me something."

"I already gave you *something* at the swimming hole."

"Yeah, but I couldn't see anything." He went right back to undoing her buttons. "I want to see you, Ash. It's been too long. I missed you."

Ash grinned. Hard not to when the man she'd fallen for was admitting to pretty much the same thing. She let him finish undoing her buttons and stood completely still as he unclasped her bra. Her hands strayed to her jeans, unsnapping the button after her bra had slipped to the floor.

"Leave your panties on," Colt commanded as she pushed her jeans down her legs. "I'll take those off at my own leisure."

When Colton picked her up and carried her to his room, she felt like she'd died and gone to heaven. She'd never felt so secure as she did, nestled against Colton's broad chest, loving the way his voice rumbled around inside, making delicious vibrations against her cheek. She felt so well cared for when he gently laid her out on the bed, and she rubbed her knees together in delighted anticipation, knowing he might not be so gentle in an hour's time.

"Roll onto your stomach," he said. "I'm going to give you a full-body massage."

"You are?"

"I once promised, and I always follow through on my promises."

Ash collapsed onto her stomach, turning her head to the side and enjoying the sight of Colton removing his clothing, realizing that what he said was the truth. He'd never lied to her. When he said he was going to do something, he did it.

He was the best man she'd ever known, and the fact he was now naked and crawling up onto the bed to straddle her made her shiver. Equally good was the warm drip of oil followed by Colton's strong hands working the oil into her skin.

"So…what is it about you and coconut oil?"

"The smell makes me randy."

"Is there a reason?"

"Do you really want to know?"

"Yes."

"There was this guy…"

"Okay. Stop."

"We met on holiday."

"I said, stop, Ash."

"He was Spanish."

Colton smacked her ass. "If you ever talk about being with another guy again, I'm going to lose it."

Ash rolled onto her back, grabbed Colton's shoulders and pulled him down on top of her. "There were basically no other men before you, Colton Cross."

"Now that's a lie I can live with."

She kissed him full on the mouth. He kissed her back softly before pausing. "Ash?"

"Yeah?"

"I know this is still pretty new, but I don't know, I've never felt this way about anyone before."

Ash almost teased him about proposing again but stopped herself when she saw how serious Colton's expression was. She swallowed down her sarcasm and refused to put up her standard defenses she'd created over the years to protect herself. "I've never felt this way before, either. Not even close," she admitted instead.

"What are we going to do?" He stroked the hair away

from her forehead. "I can quit the tour. Or maybe you can come along with me. I mean, you can do your photo blog from anywhere, right?"

"Yeah, but didn't you hear?"

"Hear what?"

"I've been given a contract with NBRA."

"Are you shitting me?"

"Nope. It's just for six months, but it means I'll be at all the pro events."

"You don't say."

"I do."

"So you're saying we're going to be on the tour, together? Living our dreams?"

"Yep."

He kissed her. It was passionate and warm and soft and sexy and everything oh, so good, all at the same time.

"Thank God, because I don't want you out of my sight again." He nibbled her lip. "I hated it when you left."

"You did?"

"I did."

Ash circled Colton's nipple with her fingertip. "And I hated leaving. I even lied about having to leave."

"Ash?"

"Yeah."

"Don't lie to me again, okay?" His mouth was suckling the underside of her jaw.

"Okay." She arched into him. "It's just I was starting to feel too…"

"Too what?" Colton teased her lips gently as his hand roved up and down her body.

"Too much," she sighed.

"Of this?" His hand settled over her mound.

"It was more than that."

His fingers penetrated her damp folds, entering her. "Was it this?"

"That and more." She moaned as he withdrew his fingers.

"Ash?" He nibbled his way up the cord in her neck to her ear. "Are you saying you love me?"

Her body jerked beneath him, and Colton propped himself up on his elbow, gazing down at her. Not smug, but with great tenderness.

"I—"

"No lying now, you promised." There was the smugness she loved.

"Bastard." She smacked his ass.

"I'll take that as a yes." He settled his weight on top of her again and touched the inside of her ear with his tongue. "That was for making me propose for your own warped enjoyment." He nudged her legs apart. "And for pushing me in the water." He took her hands and held them down above her head. Then he fit himself between her thighs. "And this," he groaned into her hair as he entered her slowly, "Is because I love you, too."

* * * * *

Get 2 Free Books,
Plus 2 Free Gifts—
just for trying the Reader Service!

HARLEQUIN *Desire*

HD17

*There's no way Lola Whittaker is going to rekindle the
flames between her and sexy smoke jumper
Erik McKnight—she still hasn't forgiven him for the past.*

*Read on for a sneak preview of
UP IN FLAMES,
the newest Kira Sinclair title from Harlequin Blaze!*

"Lola. It's good to see you."

"Erik. I can't say the same."

That wasn't strictly true. Because even as anger—
anger she'd been harboring for the last six years—burst
through her, she couldn't stop her gaze from rippling
down his body.

He was bigger—pure muscle. Considering the work he
did now, that was no surprise. Smoke jumping wasn't for
weaklings. It was, however, for daredevils and adrenaline
junkies. Erik McKnight was both.

Hurt flashed through his eyes. "I'm sorry you still feel
that way."

Wow, so he'd finally issued her an apology. Hardly for
the right reasons, though.

"What are you doing here?"

"Didn't your dad or Colt tell you?"

Her anger now had a new direction. The men in her
life were all oblivious morons.

"I'm—" his gaze pulled away, focusing on the sky
behind her "—taking a couple months off."

Six years ago she would have asked for an explanation.
Today she didn't want to care, so she kept her mouth shut.

"Came home to spend some time with Mom. Your dad's letting me pick up some shifts at the station."

Lola nodded. "Well, good luck with that." Hooking her thumb over her shoulder, she said, "I'm just gonna go…"

"Do anything that gets you far away from me."

She shrugged. He wasn't wrong, but her mother had raised her to be too polite to say so.

"You look good, Lola. I…I really am glad we ran into each other."

Was he serious? Lola stared at him for several seconds, searching his face before she realized that he was. Which made the anger bubbling up inside her finally burst free.

"Did you take a hit to the head, Erik? You act like I haven't been right here for the past six years, exactly where you left me when you ran away. Ran away when my brother was lying in a hospital bed, broken and bleeding."

"Because I put him there." Erik's gruff voice whispered over her.

"You're right. You did."

"That right there is why I left. I could see it every time you looked at me."

"See what?"

"Blame." His stark expression ripped through her. A small part of her wanted to reach out to him and offer comfort.

But he was right. She did blame him. For so many things.

Don't miss
UP IN FLAMES by Kira Sinclair,
available May 2017 wherever
Harlequin® Blaze® books and ebooks are sold.

www.Harlequin.com

HBEXP0417

EXCLUSIVE LIMITED TIME OFFER AT
www.HARLEQUIN.com

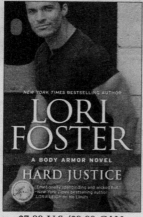

NEW YORK TIMES BESTSELLING AUTHOR

LORI FOSTER

A BODY ARMOR NOVEL

HARD JUSTICE

"Emotionally spellbinding and wicked hot."
—New York Times bestselling author
LORA LEIGH on No Limits

$7.99 U.S./$9.99 CAN.

$1.⁰⁰ OFF

New York Times Bestselling Author

LORI FOSTER

brings you the next sexy story in the
Body Armor series with

HARD JUSTICE

*Playing it safe has never felt so
dangerous…*

*Available March 21, 2017
Get your copy today!*

Receive **$1.00 OFF** the purchase price of
HARD JUSTICE by Lori Foster
when you use the coupon code below on Harlequin.com

HARDJUSTICE1

Offer valid from March 21, 2017, until April 30, 2017, on www.Harlequin.com.

Valid in the U.S.A. and Canada only. To redeem this offer, please add the print or
ebook version of HARD JUSTICE by Lori Foster to your shopping cart and then
enter the coupon code at checkout.